Rabindranath Tagore

SELECTED POEMS

COMPILED BY

PATRICIA MOORE

NEW DELHI (INDIA)

Rabindranath Tagore
SELECTED
POEMS

Published by

MG BOOKS

An Imprint of

MAANU GRAPHICS

MAANU GRAPHICS
(PUBLISHERS OF GENERAL BOOKS)
5FF, Ganpati Bhawan, 21 Ansari Road,
Darya Ganj, New Delhi-110002
Ph: 65285220, 64138266
E-mail : maanugraphics@yahoo.com
mgbooks.maanu@yahoo.com

Printed at
NEW Z. A. Printers, Delhi

CONTENTS

About the Author

Greatest writer in modern Indian literature, Bengali poet, novelist, educator, who won the Nobel Prize for Literature in 1913.

Rabindranath Tagore was born in Calcutta in a wealthy and prominent Brahman family. His father was Maharishi Debendranath Tagore, a religious reformer and scholar. His mother Sarada Devi, died when he was very young - her body carried through a gate to a place where it was burned and it was the moment when he realized that she will never come back. Tagore's grandfather had established a huge financial empire for himself, and financed public projects, such as Calcutta Medical College.

In 1883 Tagore married Mrinalini Devi Raichaudhuri, with whom he had two sons and three daughters. He moved to East Bengal in 1890.

His first book, a collection of poems, appeared when he was 17; it was published by Tagore's friend who wanted to surprise him. In East Bengal (now Bangladesh) he collected local legends and folklore and wrote seven volumes of poetry between 1893 and 1900, including Sonar Tari (The Golden Boat), 1894 and Khanika, 1900.

In 1901 Tagore founded a school outside Calcutta, Visva-Bharati, which was dedicated to emerging Western and Indian philosophy and education. It became a University in 1921. He produced poems, novels, stories, a history of India, textbooks, and treatises on pedagogy. His wife died in

1902, followed in 1903 by the death of one of his daughters and in 1907 his younger son.

Tagore's reputation as a writer was established in the United States and in England after the publication of Gitanjali: Song Offerings, in which Tagore tried to find inner calm and explored the themes of divine and human love.

The poems were translated into English by Tagore himself. His cosmic visions owed much to the lyric tradition of Vaishnava Hinduism and its concepts about the relationship between man and God. The poems appeared in 1912 with an introduction by William Butler Yates, who wrote "These lyrics - which are in the original, my Indians tell me, full of subtlety of rhythm, of untranslatable delicacies of colour, of metrical invention - display in their thought a world I have dreamed of all my life long."

His poems were praised by Ezra Pound, and drew the attention of the Nobel Prize committee.

Many of his poems are actually songs, and inseparable from their music. His written production, still not completely collected, fill 26 substantial volumes.

At the age of 70 Tagore took up painting. He was also a composer, settings hundreds of poems to music. Tagore's song Sonar Bangla Our Golden Bengal became the national anthem of Bangladesh. He was an early advocate of Independence for India and his influence over Gandhi and the founders of modern India was enormous.

FIREFLIES

I

MY fancies are fireflies—
Specks of living light
twinkling in the dark.

MY words that are slight
my lightly dance upon time's waves
when my works heavy with import have gone down.

LEAVE out my name from the gift
if it be a burden,
but keep my song.

SORROW that has lost its memory
is like the dumb dark hours
that have not bird songs

but only the cricket's chirp

THE tyrant claims freedom to kill freedom and yet to keep it for himself.

WHILE god waits for His temple to be built of love men bring stones.

II

I TOUCH GOD in my song as the hill touches the far-away sea with its waterfall.

I HAVE thanked the trees that have made my life fruitful but have failed to remember the grass that has ever kept it green.

THE WORLD suffers most from the disinterested tyranny of its well-wisher.

THESE PAPER boats of mine are meant to dance on the ripples of hours, and not to reach any destination.

III

IN THE THRILL of little leaves
I see the air's invisible dance,
and in their glimmering
the secret heart-beats of the sky.

⊹

THE WORLD speaks to me in pictures,
my soul answers in music.

⊹

LOVE IS AN endless mystery,
for it had nothing else to explain it.

⊹

I AM ABLE to love my God
because He gives me freedom to deny Him.

⊹

WEALTH IS THE burden of bigness,
Welfare the fulness of being.

IV

YOUR SMILE, my love, like the smell of a strange flower,
is simple and inexplicable.

LET ME NOT grope in vain in the dark
but keep my mind still in the faith
that the day will break
and truth will appear
in its simplicity.

LIKE MY heart's pain that has long missed its meaning,
the sun's rays robed in dark
hide themselves under the ground.
Like my heart's pain at love's sudden touch,
they change their veil at the spring's
call and come out in the carnival of colours,
in flowers and leaves.

IN MY LIFE'S garden my wealth has been of the shadows and lights that are never gathered and stored.

V

I MISS the meaning of my own part in the play of life because I know not of the parts that others play.

THE UNSEEN dark plays on his flute and the rhythm of light eddies into stars and suns, into thoughts and dreams.

WHEN the voice of the Silent touches my words I know him and therefore I know myself.

WHEN death comes and whispers to me
'Thy days are ended,'
let me say to him, 'I have lived in love
and not in mere time.'
He will ask 'Will thy songs remains?'
I shall say 'I know not, but this I know
that often when I sang if found my eternity.'

FRUIT GATHERING

I

Bid me and I shall gather my fruits to bring them in full baskets into your courtyard, though some are lost and some not ripe.

For the season grows heavy with its fulness, and there is a plaintive shepherd's pipe in the shade.

Bid me and I shall set sail on the river.

The March wind is fretful, fretting the languid waves into murmurs.

The garden has yielded its all, and in the weary hour of evening the call comes from your house on the shore in the sunset.

II

My life when young was like a flower--a flower that loosens a petal or two from her abundance and never feels the loss when the spring breeze comes to beg at her door.

Now at the end of youth my life is like a fruit, having nothing to spare, and waiting to offer herself completely with her full burden of sweetness.

III

Is summer's festival only for fresh blossoms and not also for withered leaves and faded flowers?

Is the song of the sea in tune only with the rising waves?

Does it not also sing with the waves that fall?

Jewels are woven into the carpet where stands my king, but there are patient clods waiting to be touched by his feet.

Few are the wise and the great who sit by my Master, but he has taken the foolish in his arms and made me his servant for ever.

IV

I woke and found his letter with the morning.

I do not know what it says, for I cannot read.

I shall leave the wise man alone with his books, I shall not trouble him, for who knows if he can read what the letter says.

Let me hold it to my forehead and press it to my heart.

When the night grows still and stars come out one by one I will spread it on my lap and stay silent.

The rustling leaves will read it aloud to me, the rushing stream will chant it, and the seven wise stars will sing it to me from the sky.

I cannot find what I seek, I cannot understand what I would learn; but this unread letter has lightened my burdens and turned my thoughts into songs.

V

A handful of dust could hide your signal when I did not know its meaning.

Now that I am wiser I read it in all that hid it before.

It is painted in petals of flowers; waves flash it from their foam; hills hold it high on their summits.

I had my face turned from you, therefore I read the letters awry and knew not their meaning.

VI

Where roads are made I lose my way.

In the wide water, in the blue sky there is no line of a track.

The pathway is hidden by the birds' wings, by the star-fires, by the flowers of the wayfaring seasons.

And I ask my heart if its blood carries the wisdom of the unseen way.

VII

Alas, I cannot stay in the house, and home has become no home to me, for the eternal Stranger calls, he is going along the road.

The sound of his footfall knocks at my breast; it pains me!

The wind is up, the sea is moaning. I leave all my cares and doubts to follow the homeless tide, for the Stranger calls me, he is going along the road.

VIII

Be ready to launch forth, my heart! and let those linger who must.

For your name has been called in the morning sky.

Wait for none!

The desire of the bud is for the night and dew, but the blown flower cries for the freedom of light.

Burst your sheath, my heart, and come forth!

IX

When I lingered among my hoarded treasure I felt like a worm that feeds in the dark upon the fruit where it was born.

I leave this prison of decay.

I care not to haunt the mouldy stillness, for I go in search of everlasting youth; I throw away all that is not one with my life nor as light as my laughter.

I run through time and, O my heart, in your chariot dances the poet who sings while he wanders.

X

You took my hand and drew me to your side, made me sit on the high seat before all men, till I became timid, unable to stir and walk my own way; doubting and debating at every step lest I should tread upon any thorn of their disfavour.

I am freed at last!

The blow has come, the drum of insult sounded, my seat is laid low in the dust.

My paths are open before me.

My wings are full of the desire of the sky.

I go to join the shooting stars of midnight, to plunge into the profound shadow.

I am like the storm-driven cloud of summer that, having cast off its crown of gold, hangs as a sword the thunderbolt upon a chain of lightning.

In desperate joy I run upon the dusty path of the despised; I draw near to your final welcome.

The child finds its mother when it leaves her womb.

When I am parted from you, thrown out from your household, I am free to see your face.

XI

It decks me only to mock me, this jewelled chain of mine.

It bruises me when on my neck, it strangles me when I struggle to tear it off.

It grips my throat, it chokes my singing.

Could I but offer it to your hand, my Lord, I would be saved.

Take it from me, and in exchange bind me to you with a garland, for I am ashamed to stand before you with this jewelled chain on my neck.

XII

Far below flowed the Jumna, swift and clear, above frowned the jutting bank.

Hills dark with the woods and scarred with the torrents were gathered around.

Govinda, the great Sikh teacher, sat on the rock reading scriptures, when Raghunath, his disciple, proud of his wealth, caine and bowed to him and said, "I have brought my poor present unworthy of your acceptance."

[Transcriber's note: In the above verse, the word 'caine' does not fit in, the word 'came' makes more sense]

Thus saying he displayed before the teacher a pair of gold bangles wrought with costly stones.

The master took up one of them, twirling it round his finger, and the diamonds darted shafts of light.

Suddenly it slipped from his hand and rolled down the

bank into the water.

"Alas," screamed Raghunath, and jumped into the stream.

The teacher set his eyes upon his book, and the water held and hid what it stole and went its way.

The daylight faded when Raghunath came back to the teacher tired and dripping.

He panted and said, "I can still get it back if you show me where it fell."

The teacher took up the remaining bangle and throwing it into the water said, "It is there."

XIII

To move is to meet you every moment, Fellow-traveller!

It is to sing to the falling of your feet.

He whom your breath touches does not glide by the shelter of the bank.

He spreads a reckless sail to the wind and rides the turbulent water.

He who throws his doors open and steps onward receives your greeting.

He does not stay to count his gain or to mourn his loss; his heart beats the drum for his march, for that is to march with you every step,

Fellow-traveller!

XIV

My portion of the best in this world will come from your hands: such was your promise.

Therefore your light glistens in my tears.

I fear to be led by others lest I miss you waiting in some road corner to be my guide.

I walk my own wilful way till my very folly tempts you to my door.

For I have your promise that my portion of the best in this world will come from your hands.

XV

Your speech is simple, my Master, but not theirs who talk of you.

I understand the voice of your stars and the silence of your trees.

I know that my heart would open like a flower; that my life has filled itself at a hidden fountain.

Your songs, like birds from the lonely land of snow, are winging to build their nests in my heart against the warmth of its April, and I am content to wait for the merry season.

XVI

They knew the way and went to seek you along the narrow lane, but I wandered abroad into the night for I was ignorant.

I was not schooled enough to be afraid of you in the dark, therefore I came upon your doorstep unaware:

The wise rebuked me and bade me be gone, for I had not come by the lane.

I turned away in doubt, but you held me fast, and their scolding became louder every day.

XVII

I brought out my earthen lamp from my house and cried, "Come, children, I will light your path!"

The night was still dark when I returned, leaving the road to its silence, crying, "Light me, O Fire! for my earthen lamp lies broken in the dust!"

XVIII

No: it is not yours to open buds into blossoms.

Shake the bud, strike it; it is beyond your power to make it blossom.

Your touch soils it, you tear its petals to pieces and strew them in the dust.

But no colours appear, and no perfume.

Ah! it is not for you to open the bud into a blossom.

He who can open the bud does it so simply.

He gives it a glance, and the life-sap stirs through its veins.

At his breath the flower spreads its wings and flutters in the wind.

Colours flush out like heart-longings, the perfume betrays a sweet secret.

He who can open the bud does it so simply.

XIX

Sudâs, the gardener, plucked from his tank the last lotus left by the ravage of winter and went to sell it to the king at the palace gate.

There he met a traveller who said to him, "Ask your price for the last lotus, --I shall offer it to Lord Buddha."

Sudâs said, "If you pay one golden mâshâ it will be yours.

The traveller paid it.

At that moment the king came out and he wished to buy the flower, for he was on his way to see Lord Buddha, and he thought, "It would be a fine thing to lay at his feet the lotus that bloomed in winter."

When the gardener said he had been offered a golden mâshâ the king offered him ten, but the traveller doubled the price.

The gardener, being greedy, imagined a greater gain from him for whose sake they were bidding. He bowed and said, "I cannot sell this lotus."

In the hushed shade of the mango grove beyond the city wall Sudâs stood before Lord Buddha, on whose lips sat the silence of love and whose eyes beamed peace like the morning star of the dew-washed autumn.

Sudâs looked in his face and put the lotus at his feet and bowed his head to the dust.

Buddha smiled and asked, "What is your wish, my son?"

Sudâs cried, "The least touch of your feet."

XX

Make me thy poet, O Night, veiled Night!

There are some who have sat speechless for ages in thy shadow; let me utter their songs.

Take me up on thy chariot without wheels, running noiselessly from world to world, thou queen in the palace of time, thou darkly beautiful!

Many a questioning mind has stealthily entered thy courtyard and roamed through thy lampless house seeking for answers.

From many a heart, pierced with the arrow of joy from the hands of the Unknown, have burst forth glad chants, shaking the darkness to its foundation.

Those wakeful souls gaze in the starlight in wonder at the treasure they have suddenly found.

Make me their poet, O Night, the poet of thy fathomless silence.

XXI

I will meet one day the Life within me, the joy that hides in my life, though the days perplex my path with their idle dust.

I have known it in glimpses, and its fitful breath has come upon me, making my thoughts fragrant for a while.

I will meet one day the Joy without me that dwells behind the screen of light--and will stand in the overflowing solitude where all things are seen as by their creator.

XXII

This autumn morning is tired with excess of light, and if your songs grow fitful and languid give me your flute awhile.

I shall but play with it as the whim takes me,--now take it on my lap, now touch it with my lips, now keep it by my side on the grass.

But in the solemn evening stillness I shall gather flowers, to deck it with wreaths, I shall fill it with fragrance; I shall worship it with the lighted lamp.

Then at night I shall come to you and give you back your flute.

You will play on it the music of midnight when the lonely crescent moon wanders among the stars.

XXIII

The poet's mind floats and dances on the waves of life amidst the voices of wind and water.

Now when the sun has set and the darkened sky draws upon the sea like drooping lashes upon a weary eye it is time to take away his pen, and let his thoughts sink into the bottom of the deep amid the eternal secret of that silence.

XXIV

The night is dark and your slumber is deep in the hush of my being.

Wake, O Pain of Love, for I know not how to open the door, and I stand outside.

The hours wait, the stars watch, the wind is still, the silence is heavy in my heart.

Wake, Love, wake! brim my empty cup, and with a breath of song ruffle the night.

XXV

The bird of the morning sings.

Whence has he word of the morning before the morning breaks, and when the dragon night still holds the sky in its cold black coils?

Tell me, bird of the morning, how, through the twofold

night of the sky and the leaves, he found his way into your dream, the messenger out of the east?

The world did not believe you when you cried, "The sun is on his way, the night is no more."

O sleeper, awake!

Bare your forehead, waiting for the first blessing of light, and sing with the bird of the morning in glad faith.

XXVI

The beggar in me lifted his lean hands to the starless sky and cried into night's ear with his hungry voice.

His prayers were to the blind Darkness who lay like a fallen god in a desolate heaven of lost hopes.

The cry of desire eddied round a chasm of despair, a wailing bird circling its empty nest.

But when morning dropped anchor at the rim of the East, the beggar in me leapt and cried:

"Blessed am I that the deaf night denied me--that its coffer was empty."

He cried, "O Life, O Light, you are precious! and precious is the joy that at last has known you!"

XXVII

Sanâtan was telling his beads by the Ganges when a Brahmin in rags came to him and said, "Help me, I am poor!"

"My alms-bowl is all that is my own," said Sanâtan, "I have given away everything I had."

"But my lord Shiva came to me in my dreams," said the Brahmin, "and counselled me to come to you."

Sanâtan suddenly remembered he had picked up a stone without price among the pebbles on the river-bank, and thinking that some one might need it hid it in the sands.

He pointed out the spot to the Brahmin, who wondering dug up the stone.

The Brahmin sat on the earth and mused alone till the sun went down behind the trees, and cowherds went home with their cattle.

Then he rose and came slowly to Sanâtan and said, "Master, give me the least fraction of the wealth that disdains all the wealth of the world."

And he threw the precious stone into the water.

XXVIII

Time after time I came to your gate with raised hands, asking for more and yet more.

You gave and gave, now in slow measure, now in sudden excess.

I took some, and some things I let drop; some lay heavy on my hands; some I made into playthings and broke them when tired; till the wrecks and the hoard of your gifts grew immense, hiding you, and the ceaseless expectation wore my heart out.

Take, oh take--has now become my cry.

Shatter all from this beggar's bowl: put out this lamp of

the importunate watcher: hold my hands, raise me from the still-gathering heap of your gifts into the bare infinity of your uncrowded presence.

XXIX

You have set me among those who are defeated.

I know it is not for me to win, nor to leave the game.

I shall plunge into the pool although but to sink to the bottom.

I shall play the game of my undoing.

I shall stake all I have and when I lose my last penny I shall stake myself, and then I think I shall have won through my utter defeat.

XXX

A smile of mirth spread over the sky when you dressed my heart in rags and sent her forth into the road to beg.

She went from door to door, and many a time when her bowl was nearly full she was robbed.

At the end of the weary day she came to your palace gate holding up her pitiful bowl, and you came and took her hand and seated her beside you on your throne.

XXXI

"Who among you will take up the duty of feeding the hungry?" Lord Buddha asked his followers when famine raged at Shravasti.

Ratnâkar, the banker, hung his head and said, "Much more is needed than all my wealth to feed the hungry."

Jaysen, the chief of the King's army, said, "I would gladly give my life's blood, but there is not enough food in my house."

Dharmapâal, who owned broad acres of land, said with a sigh, "The drought demon has sucked my fields dry. I know not how to pay King's dues."

Then rose Supriyâ, the mendicant's daughter.

She bowed to all and meekly said, "I will feed the hungry."

"How!" they cried in surprise. "How can you hope to fulfil that vow?"

"I am the poorest of you all," said Supriyâ, "that is my strength. I have my coffer and my store at each of your houses."

XXXII

My king was unknown to me, therefore when he claimed his tribute I was bold to think I would hide myself leaving my debts unpaid.

I fled and fled behind my day's work and my night's dreams.

But his claims followed me at every breath I drew.

Thus I came to know that I am known to him and no place left which is mine.

Now I wish to lay my all before his feet, and gain the right to my place in his kingdom.

XXXIII

When I thought I would mould you, an image from my life for men to worship, I brought my dust and desires and all my coloured delusions and dreams.

When I asked you to mould with my life an image from your heart for you to love, you brought your fire and force, and truth, loveliness and peace.

XXXIV

"Sire," announced the servant to the King, "the saint Narottam has never deigned to enter your royal temple.

"He is singing God's praise under the trees by the open road. The temple is empty of worshippers.

"They flock round him like bees round the white lotus, leaving the golden jar of honey unheeded."

The King, vexed at heart, went to the spot where Narottam sat on the grass.

He asked him, "Father, why leave my temple of the golden dome and sit on the dust outside to preach God's love?"

"Because God is not there in your temple," said Narottam.

The King frowned and said, "Do you know, twenty

millions of gold went to the making of that marvel of art, and it was consecrated to God with costly rites?"

"Yes, I know it," answered Narottam. "It was in that year when thousands of your people whose houses had been burned stood vainly asking for help at your door.

"And God said, 'The poor creature who can give no shelter to his brothers would build my house!'

"And he took his place with the shelterless under the trees by the road.

"And that golden bubble is empty of all but hot vapour of pride."

The King cried in anger, "Leave my land."

Calmly said the saint, "Yes, banish me where you have banished my God."

XXXV

The trumpet lies in the dust.

The wind is weary, the light is dead.

Ah, the evil day!

Come, fighters, carrying your flags, and singers, with your war-songs!

Come, pilgrims of the march, hurrying on your journey!

The trumpet lies in the dust waiting for us.

I was on my way to the temple with my evening offerings, seeking for a place of rest after the day's dusty toil: hoping my hurts would be healed and the stains in my garment washed white, when I found thy trumpet lying in the dust.

Was it not the hour for me to light my evening lamp?

Had not the night sung its lullaby to the stars?

O thou blood-red rose, my poppies of sleep have paled and faded!

I was certain my wanderings were over and my debts all paid when suddenly I came upon thy trumpet lying in the dust.

Strike my drowsy heart with thy spell of youth!

Let my joy in life blaze up in fire. Let the shafts of awakening fly through the heart of night, and a thrill of dread shake blindness and palsy.

I have come to raise thy trumpet from the dust.

Sleep is no more for me--my walk shall be through showers of arrows.

Some shall run out of their houses and come to my side--some shall weep.

Some in their beds shall toss and groan in dire dreams.

For to-night thy trumpet shall be sounded.

From thee I have asked peace only to find shame.

Now I stand before thee--help me to put on my armour!

Let hard blows of trouble strike fire into my life.

Let my heart beat in pain, the drum of thy victory.

My hands shall be utterly emptied to take up thy trumpet.

XXXVI

When, mad in their mirth, they raised dust to soil thy robe, O Beautiful, it made my heart sick.

I cried to thee and said, "Take thy rod of punishment and

judge them."

The morning light struck upon those eyes, red with the revel of night; the place of the white lily greeted their burning breath; the stars through the depth of the sacred dark stared at their carousing--at those that raised dust to soil thy robe, O Beautiful!

Thy judgment seat was in the flower garden, in the birds' notes in springtime: in the shady river-banks, where the trees muttered in answer to the muttering of the waves.

O my Lover, they were pitiless in their passion.

They prowled in the dark to snatch thy ornaments to deck their own desires.

When they had struck thee and thou wert pained, it pierced me to the quick, and I cried to thee and said, "Take thy sword, O my Lover, and judge them!"

Ah, but thy justice was vigilant.

A mother's tears were shed on their insolence; the imperishable faith of a lover hid their spears of rebellion in its own wounds.

Thy judgment was in the mute pain of sleepless love: in the blush of the chaste: in the tears of the night of the desolate: in the pale morning-light of forgiveness.

O Terrible, they in their reckless greed climbed thy gate at night, breaking into thy storehouse to rob thee.

But the weight of their plunder grew immense, too heavy to carry or to remove.

Thereupon I cried to thee and said, Forgive them, O Terrible!

Thy forgiveness burst in storms, throwing them down, scattering their thefts in the dust.

Thy forgiveness was in the thunder-stone; in the shower of blood; in the angry red of the sunset.

XXXVII

Upagupta, the disciple of Buddha, lay asleep on the dust by the city wall of Mathura.

Lamps were all out, doors were all shut, and stars were all hidden by the murky sky of August.

Whose feet were those tinkling with anklets, touching his breast of a sudden?

He woke up startled, and the light from a woman's lamp struck his forgiving eyes.

It was the dancing girl, starred with jewels, clouded with a pale-blue mantle, drunk with the wine of her youth.

She lowered her lamp and saw the young face, austerely beautiful.

"Forgive me, young ascetic," said the woman; "graciously come to my house. The dusty earth is not a fit bed for you."

The ascetic answered, "Woman, go on your way; when the time is ripe I will come to you."

Suddenly the black night showed its teeth in a flash of lightning.

The storm growled from the corner of the sky, and the woman trembled in fear.

The branches of the wayside trees were aching with blossom.

Gay notes of the flute came floating in the warm spring air from afar.

The citizens had gone to the woods, to the festival of flowers.

From the mid-sky gazed the full moon on the shadows of the silent town.

The young ascetic was walking in the lonely street, while overhead the lovesick koels urged from the mango branches their sleepless plaint.

Upagupta passed through the city gates, and stood at the base of the rampart.

What woman lay in the shadow of the wall at his feet, struck with the black pestilence, her body spotted with sores, hurriedly driven away from the town?

The ascetic sat by her side, taking her head on his knees, and moistened her lips with water and smeared her body with balm.

"Who are you, merciful one?" asked the woman.

"The time, at last, has come to visit you, and I am here," replied the young ascetic.

XXXVIII

This is no mere dallying of love between us, my lover.

Again and again have swooped down upon me the screaming nights of storm, blowing out my lamp: dark doubts have gathered, blotting out all stars from my sky.

Again and again the banks have burst, letting the flood sweep away my harvest, and wailing and despair have rent my sky from end to end.

This have I learnt that there are blows of pain in your love, never the cold apathy of death.

XXXIX

The wall breaks asunder, light, like divine laughter, bursts in. Victory, O Light!

The heart of the night is pierced!

With your flashing sword cut in twain the tangle of doubt and feeble desires!

Victory!

Come, Implacable!

Come, you who are terrible in your whiteness.

O Light, your drum sounds in the march of fire, and the red torch is held on high; death dies in a burst of splendour!

XL

O fire, my brother, I sing victory to you.

You are the bright red image of fearful freedom.

You swing your arms in the sky, you sweep your impetuous fingers across the harp-string, your dance music is beautiful.

When my days are ended and the gates are opened you will burn to ashes this cordage of hands and feet.

My body will be one with you, my heart will be caught in the whirls of your frenzy, and the burning heat that was my life will flash up and mingle itself in your flame.

XLI

The Boatman is out crossing the wild sea at night.

The mast is aching because of its full sails filled with the violent wind.

Stung with the night's fang the sky falls upon the sea, poisoned with black fear.

The waves dash their heads against the dark unseen, and the Boatman is out crossing the wild sea.

The Boatman is out, I know not for what tryst, startling the night with the sudden white of his sails.

I know not at what shore, at last, he lands to reach the silent courtyard where the lamp is burning and to find her who sits in the dust and waits.

What is the quest that makes his boat care not for storm nor darkness?

Is it heavy with gems and pearls?

Ah, no, the Boatman brings with him no treasure, but only a white rose in his hand and a song on his lips.

It is for her who watches alone at night with her lamp burning.

She dwells in the wayside hut. Her loose hair flies in the wind and hides her eyes.

The storm shrieks through her broken doors, the light flickers in her earthen lamp flinging shadows on the walls.

Through the howl of the winds she hears him call her

name, she whose name is unknown.

It is long since the Boatman sailed. It will be long before the day breaks and he knocks at the door.

The drums will not be beaten and none will know.

Only light shall fill the house, blessed shall be the dust, and the heart glad.

All doubts shall vanish in silence when the Boatman comes to the shore.

XLII

I cling to this living raft, my body, in the narrow stream of my earthly years.

I leave it when the crossing is over. And then?

I do not know if the light there and the darkness are the same.

The Unknown is the perpetual freedom:

He is pitiless in his love.

He crushes the shell for the pearl, dumb in the prison of the dark.

You muse and weep for the days that are done, poor heart!

Be glad that days are to come!

The hour strikes, O pilgrim!

It is time for you to take the parting of the ways!

His face will be unveiled once again and you shall meet.

XLIII

Over the relic of Lord Buddha King Bimbisâr built a shrine, a salutation in white marble.

There in the evening would come all the brides and daughters of the King's house to offer flowers and light lamps.

When the son became king in his time he washed his father's creed away with blood, and lit sacrificial fires with its sacred books.

The autumn day was dying. The evening hour of worship was near.

Shrimati, the queen's maid, devoted to Lord Buddha, having bathed in holy water, and decked the golden tray with lamps and fresh white blossoms, silently raised her dark eyes to the queen's face.

The queen shuddered in fear and said, "Do you not know, foolish girl, that death is the penalty for whoever brings worship to Buddha's shrine?

"Such is the king's will."

Shrimati bowed to the queen, and turning away from her door came and stood before Amitâ, the newly wed bride of the king's son.

A mirror of burnished gold on her lap, the newly wed bride was braiding her dark long tresses and painting the red spot of good luck at the parting of her hair.

Her hands trembled when she saw the young maid, and she cried, "What fearful peril would you bring me! Leave me this instant."

Princess Shuklâ sat at the window reading her book of romance by the light of the setting sun.

She started when she saw at her door the maid with the sacred offerings.

Her book fell down from her lap, and she whispered in Shrimati's ears, "Rush not to death, daring woman!"

Shrimati walked from door to door. She raised her head and cried, "O women of the king's house, hasten!

"The time for our Lord's worship is come!"

Some shut their doors in her face and some reviled her.

The last gleam of daylight faded from the bronze dome of the palace tower.

Deep shadows settled in street corners: the bustle of the city was hushed: the gong at the temple of Shiva announced the time of the evening prayer.

In the dark of the autumn evening, deep as a limpid lake, stars throbbed with light, when the guards of the palace garden were startled to see through the trees a row of lamps burning at the shrine of Buddha.

They ran with their swords unsheathed, crying, "Who are you, foolish one, reckless of death?"

"I am Shrimati," replied a sweet voice, "the servant of Lord Buddha."

The next moment her heart's blood coloured the cold marble with its red.

And in the still hour of stars died the light of the last lamp of worship at the foot of the shrine.

XLIV

The day that stands between you and me makes her last bow of farewell.

The night draws her veil over her face, and hides the one lamp burning in my chamber.

Your dark servant comes noiselessly and spreads the bridal carpet for you to take your seat there alone with me in the wordless silence till night is done.

XLV

My night has passed on the bed of sorrow, and my eyes are tired. My heavy heart is not yet ready to meet morning with its crowded joys.

Draw a veil over this naked light, beckon aside from me this glaring flash and dance of life.

Let the mantle of tender darkness cover me in its folds, and cover my pain awhile from the pressure of the world.

XLVI

The time is past when I could repay her for all that I received.

Her night has found its morning and thou hast taken her to thy arms: and to thee I bring my gratitude and my gifts that were for her.

For all hurts and offences to her I come to thee for

forgiveness.

I offer to thy service those flowers of my love that remained in bud when she waited for them to open.

XLVII

I found a few old letters of mine carefully hidden in her box--a few small toys for her memory to play with.

With a timorous heart she tried to steal these trifles from time's turbulent stream, and said, "These are mine only!"

Ah, there is no one now to claim them, who can pay their price with loving care, yet here they are still.

Surely there is love in this world to save her from utter loss, even like this love of hers that saved these letters with such fond care.

XLVIII

Bring beauty and order into my forlorn life, woman, as you brought them into my house when you lived.

Sweep away the dusty fragments of the hours, fill the empty jars, and mend all that has been neglected.

Then open the inner door of the shrine, light the candle, and let us meet there in silence before our God.

XLIX

The pain was great when the strings were being tuned, my Master!

Begin your music, and let me forget the pain; let me feel in beauty what you had in your mind through those pitiless days.

The waning night lingers at my doors, let her take her leave in songs.

Pour your heart into my life strings, my Master, in tunes that descend from your stars.

L

In the lightning flash of a moment I have seen the immensity of your creation in my life--creation through many a death from world to world.

I weep at my unworthiness when I see my life in the hands of the unmeaning hours,--but when I see it in your hands I know it is too precious to be squandered among shadows.

LI

I know that at the dim end of some day the sun will bid me its farewell.

Shepherds will play their pipes beneath the banyan trees,

and cattle graze on the slope by the river, while my days will pass into the dark.

This is my prayer, that I may know before I leave why the earth called me to her arms.

Why her night's silence spoke to me of stars, and her daylight kissed my thoughts into flower.

Before I go may I linger over my last refrain, completing its music, may the lamp be lit to see your face and the wreath woven to crown you.

LII

What music is that in whose measure the world is rocked?

We laugh when it beats upon the crest of life, we shrink in terror when it returns into the dark.

But the play is the same that comes and goes with the rhythm of the endless music.

You hide your treasure in the palm of your hand, and we cry that we are robbed.

But open and shut your palm as you will, the gain and the loss are the same.

At the game you play with your own self you lose and win at once.

LIII

I have kissed this world with my eyes and my limbs; I have wrapt it within my heart in numberless folds; I have flooded its days and nights with thoughts till the world and my life have grown one,--and I love my life because I love the light of the sky so enwoven with me.

If to leave this world be as real as to love it--then there must be a meaning in the meeting and the parting of life.

If that love were deceived in death, then the canker of this deceit would eat into all things, and the stars would shrivel and grow black.

LIV

The Cloud said to me, "I vanish"; the Night said, "I plunge into the fiery dawn."

The Pain said, "I remain in deep silence as his footprint."

"I die into the fulness," said my life to me.

The Earth said, "My lights kiss your thoughts every moment."

"The days pass," Love said, "but I wait for you."

Death said, "I ply the boat of your life across the sea."

LV

Tulsidas, the poet, was wandering, deep in thought, by the Ganges, in that lonely spot where they burn their dead.

He found a woman sitting at the feet of the corpse of her dead husband, gaily dressed as for a wedding.

She rose as she saw him, bowed to him, and said, "Permit

me, Master, with your blessing, to follow my husband to heaven."

"Why such hurry, my daughter?" asked Tulsidas. "Is not this earth also His who made heaven?"

"For heaven I do not long," said the woman. "I want my husband."

Tulsidas smiled and said to her, "Go back to your home, my child. Before the month is over you will find your husband."

The woman went back with glad hope. Tulsidas came to her every day and gave her high thoughts to think, till her heart was filled to the brim with divine love.

When the month was scarcely over, her neighbours came to her, asking, "Woman, have you found your husband?"

The widow smiled and said, "I have."

Eagerly they asked, "Where is he?"

"In my heart is my lord, one with me," said the woman.

LVI

You came for a moment to my side and touched me with the great mystery of the woman that there is in the heart of creation.

She who is ever returning to God his own outflowing of sweetness; she is the ever fresh beauty and youth in nature; she dances in the bubbling streams and sings in the morning light; she with heaving waves suckles the thirsty earth; in her the Eternal One breaks in two in a joy that no longer may contain itself, and overflows in the pain of love.

LVII

Who is she who dwells in my heart, the woman forlorn for ever?

I wooed her and I failed to win her. I decked her with wreaths and sang in her praise.

A smile shone in her face for a moment, then it faded.

"I have no joy in thee," she cried, the woman in sorrow.

I bought her jewelled anklets and fanned her with a fan gem-studded; I made her a bed on a bedstead of gold.

There flickered a gleam of gladness in her eyes, then it died.

"I have no joy in these," she cried, the woman in sorrow.

I seated her upon a car of triumph and drove her from end to end of the earth.

Conquered hearts bowed down at her feet, and shouts of applause rang in the sky.

Pride shone in her eyes for a moment, then it was dimmed in tears.

"I have no joy in conquest," she cried, the woman in sorrow.

I asked her, "Tell me whom do you seek?"

She only said, "I wait for him of the unknown name."

Days pass by and she cries, "When will my beloved come whom I know not, and be known to me for ever?"

LVIII

Yours is the light that breaks forth from the dark, and the good that sprouts from the cleft heart of strife.

Yours is the house that opens upon the world, and the love that calls to the battlefield.

Yours is the gift that still is a gain when everything is a loss, and the life that flows through the caverns of death.

Yours is the heaven that lies in the common dust, and you are there for me, you are there for all.

LIX

When the weariness of the road is upon me, and the thirst of the sultry day; when the ghostly hours of the dusk throw their shadows across my life, then I cry not for your voice only, my friend, but for your touch.

There is an anguish in my heart for the burden of its riches not given to you.

Put out your hand through the night, let me hold it and fill it and keep it; let me feel its touch along the lengthening stretch of my loneliness.

LX

The odour cries in the bud, "Ah me, the day departs, the happy day of spring, and I am a prisoner in petals!"

Do not lose heart, timid thing! Your bonds will burst, the bud will open into flower, and when you die in the fulness of life, even then the spring will live on.

The odour pants and flutters within the bud, crying, "Ah me, the hours pass by, yet I do not know where I go, or what it is I seek!"

Do not lose heart, timid thing! The spring breeze has overheard your desire, the day will not end before you have fulfilled your being.

Dark is the future to her, and the odour cries in despair, "Ah me, through whose fault is my life so unmeaning?

"Who can tell me, why I am at all?" Do not lose heart, timid thing! The perfect dawn is near when you will mingle your life with all life and know at last your purpose.

LXI

She is still a child, my lord.

She runs about your palace and plays, and tries to make of you a plaything as well.

She heeds not when her hair tumbles down and her careless garment drags in the dust.

She falls asleep when you speak to her and answers not--and the flower you give her in the morning slips to the dust from her hands.

When the storm bursts and darkness is over the sky she is sleepless; her dolls lie scattered on the earth and she clings to you in terror.

She is afraid that she may fail in service to you.

But with a smile you watch her at her game.

You know her.

The child sitting in the dust is your destined bride; her play will be stilled and deepened into love.

LXII

"What is there but the sky, O Sun, that can hold thine image?"

"I dream of thee, but to serve thee I can never hope," the dewdrop wept and said, "I am too small to take thee unto me, great lord, and my life is all tears."

"I illumine the limitless sky, yet I can yield myself up to a tiny drop of dew," thus the Sun said; "I shall become but a sparkle of light and fill you, and your little life will be a laughing orb."

LXIII

Not for me is the love that knows no restraint, but like the foaming wine that having burst its vessel in a moment would run to waste.

Send me the love which is cool and pure like your rain that blesses the thirsty earth and fills the homely earthen jars.

Send me the love that would soak down into the centre of being, and from there would spread like the unseen sap through the branching tree of life, giving birth to fruits and flowers.

Send me the love that keeps the heart still with the fulness of peace.

LXIV

The sun had set on the western margin of the river among the tangle of the forest.

The hermit boys had brought the cattle home, and sat round the fire to listen to the master, Guatama, when a strange boy came, and greeted him with fruits and flowers, and, bowing low at his feet, spoke in a bird-like voice--"Lord, I have come to thee to be taken into the path of the supreme Truth.

"My name is Satyakâma."

"Blessings be on thy head," said the master.

"Of what clan art thou, my child? It is only fitting for a Brahmin to aspire to the highest wisdom."

"Master," answered the boy, "I know not of what clan I am. I shall go and ask my mother."

Thus saying, Satyakâma took leave, and wading across the shallow stream, came back to his mother's hut, which stood at the end of the sandy waste at the edge of the sleeping village.

The lamp burnt dimly in the room, and the mother stood at the door in the dark waiting for her son's return.

She clasped him to her bosom, kissed him on his hair, and asked him of his errand to the master.

"What is the name of my father, dear mother?" asked the boy.

"It is only fitting for a Brahmin to aspire to the highest wisdom, said Lord Guatama to me."

The woman lowered her eyes, and spoke in a whisper.

"In my youth I was poor and had many masters. Thou didst come to thy mother Jabâlâ's arms, my darling, who had no husband."

The early rays of the sun glistened on the tree-tops of the forest hermitage.

The students, with their tangled hair still wet with their morning bath, sat under the ancient tree, before the master.

There came Satyakâma.

He bowed low at the feet of the sage, and stood silent.

"Tell me," the great teacher asked him, "of what clan art thou?"

"My lord," he answered, "I know it not. My mother said when I asked her, 'I had served many masters in my youth, and thou hadst come to thy mother Jabâlâ's arms, who had no husband.'"

There rose a murmur like the angry hum of bees disturbed in their hive; and the students muttered at the shameless insolence of that outcast.

Master Guatama rose from his seat, stretched out his arms, took the boy to his bosom, and said, "Best of all Brahmins art thou, my child. Thou hast the noblest heritage of truth."

LXV

May be there is one house in this city where the gate opens for ever this morning at the touch of the sunrise, where the errand of the light is fulfilled.

The flowers have opened in hedges and gardens, and may

be there is one heart that has found in them this morning the gift that has been on its voyage from endless time.

LXVI

Listen, my heart, in his flute is the music of the smell of wild flowers, of the glistening leaves and gleaming water, of shadows resonant with bees' wings.

The flute steals his smile from my friend's lips and spreads it over my life.

LXVII

You always stand alone beyond the stream of my songs.

The waves of my tunes wash your feet but I know not how to reach them.

This play of mine with you is a play from afar.

It is the pain of separation that melts into melody through my flute.

I wait for the time when your boat crosses over to my shore and you take my flute into your own hands.

LXVIII

Suddenly the window of my heart flew open this morning, the window that looks out on your heart.

I wondered to see that the name by which you know me is written in April leaves and flowers, and I sat silent.

The curtain was blown away for a moment between my songs and yours.

I found that your morning light was full of my own mute songs unsung; I thought that I would learn them at your feet--and I sat silent.

LXIX

You were in the centre of my heart, therefore when my heart wandered she never found you; you hid yourself from my loves and hopes till the last, for you were always in them.

You were the inmost joy in the play of my youth, and when I was too busy with the play the joy was passed by.

You sang to me in the ecstasies of my life and I forgot to sing to you.

LXX

When you hold your lamp in the sky it throws its light on my face and its shadow falls over you.

When I hold the lamp of love in my heart its light falls on you and I am left standing behind in the shadow.

LXXI

O the waves, the sky-devouring waves, glistening with light, dancing with life, the waves of eddying joy, rushing for ever.

The stars rock upon them, thoughts of every tint are cast up out of the deep and scattered on the beach of life.

Birth and death rise and fall with their rhythm, and the sea-gull of my heart spreads its wings crying in delight.

LXXII

The joy ran from all the world to build my body.

The lights of the skies kissed and kissed her till she woke.

Flowers of hurrying summers sighed in her breath and voices of winds and water sang in her movements.

The passion of the tide of colours in clouds and in forests flowed into her life, and the music of all things caressed her limbs into shape.

She is my bride,--she has lighted her lamp in my house.

LXXIII

The spring with its leaves and flowers has come into my body.

The bees hum there the morning long, and the winds idly play with the shadows.

A sweet fountain springs up from the heart of my heart.

My eyes are washed with delight like the dew-bathed morning, and life is quivering in all my limbs like the sounding strings of the lute.

Are you wandering alone by the shore of my life, where the tide is in flood, O lover of my endless days?

Are my dreams flitting round you like the moths with their many-coloured wings?

And are those your songs that are echoing in the dark eaves of my being?

Who but you can hear the hum of the crowded hours that sounds in my veins to-day, the glad steps that dance in my breast, the clamour of the restless life beating its wings in my body?

LXXIV

My bonds are cut, my debts are paid, my door has been opened, I go everywhere.

They crouch in their corner and weave their web of pale hours, they count their coins sitting in the dust and call me back.

But my sword is forged, my armour is put on, my horse is eager to run.

I shall win my kingdom.

LXXV

It was only the other day that I came to your earth, naked and nameless, with a wailing cry.

To-day my voice is glad, while you, my lord, stand aside to make room that I may fill my life.

Even when I bring you my songs for an offering I have the secret hope that men will come and love me for them.

You love to discover that I love this world where you have brought me.

LXXVI

Timidly I cowered in the shadow of safety, but now, when the surge of joy carries my heart upon its crest, my heart clings to the cruel rock of its trouble.

I sat alone in a corner of my house thinking it too narrow for any guest, but now when its door is flung open by an unbidden joy I find there is room for thee and for all the world.

I walked upon tiptoe, careful of my person, perfumed, and adorned--but now when a glad whirlwind has overthrown me in the dust I laugh and roll on the earth at thy feet like a child.

LXXVII

The world is yours at once and for ever.

And because you have no want, my king, you have no pleasure in your wealth.

It is as though it were naught. Therefore through slow time you give me what is yours, and ceaselessly win your kingdom in me.

Day after day you buy your sunrise from my heart, and you find your love carven into the image of my life.

LXXVIII

To the birds you gave songs, the birds gave you songs in return.

You gave me only voice, yet asked for more, and I sing.

You made your winds light and they are fleet in their service. You burdened my hands that I myself may lighten them, and at last, gain unburdened freedom for your service.

You created your Earth filling its shadows with fragments of light.

There you paused; you left me empty-handed in the dust to create your heaven.

To all things else you give; from me you ask.

The harvest of my life ripens in the sun and the shower till I reap more than you sowed, gladdening your heart, O Master of the golden granary.

LXXIX

Let me not pray to be sheltered from dangers but to be fearless in facing them.

Let me not beg for the stilling of my pain but for the heart to conquer it.

Let me not look for allies in life's battlefield but to my own strength.

Let me not crave in anxious fear to be saved but hope for the patience to win my freedom.

Grant me that I may not be a coward, feeling your mercy in my success alone; but let me find the grasp of your hand in my failure.

LXXX

You did not know yourself when you dwelt alone, and there was no crying of an errand when the wind ran from the hither to the farther shore.

I came and you woke, and the skies blossomed with lights.

You made me open in many flowers; rocked me in the cradles of many forms; hid me in death and found me again in life.

I came and your heart heaved; pain came to you and joy.

You touched me and tingled into love.

But in my eyes there is a film of shame and in my breast a flicker of fear; my face is veiled and I weep when I cannot see you.

Yet I know the endless thirst in your heart for sight of me, the thirst that cries at my door in the repeated knockings of sunrise.

LXXXI

You, in your timeless watch, listen to my approaching steps while your gladness gathers in the morning twilight and breaks in the burst of light.

The nearer I draw to you the deeper grows the fervour in the dance of the sea.

Your world is a branching spray of light filling your hands, but your heaven is in my secret heart; it slowly opens its buds in shy love.

LXXXII

I will utter your name, sitting alone among the shadows of my silent thoughts.

I will utter it without words, I will utter it without purpose.

For I am like a child that calls its mother an hundred times, glad that it can say "Mother."

LXXXIII

I

I feel that all the stars shine in me. The world breaks into my life like a flood.

The flowers blossom in my body. All the youthfulness of land and water smokes like an incense in my heart; and the breath of all things plays on my thoughts as on a flute.

II

When the world sleeps I come to your door.

The stars are silent, and I am afraid to sing.

I wait and watch, till your shadow passes by the balcony of night and I return with a full heart.

Then in the morning I sing by the roadside;

The flowers in the hedge give me answer and the morning air listens,

The travellers suddenly stop and look in my face, thinking I have called them by their names.

III

Keep me at your door ever attending to your wishes, and let me go about in your Kingdom accepting your call.

Let me not sink and disappear in the depth of languor.

Let not my life be worn out to tatters by penury of waste.

Let not those doubts encompass me,--the dust of distractions.

Let me not pursue many paths to gather many things.
Let me not bend my heart to the yoke of the many.
Let me hold my head high in the courage and pride of being your servant.

LXXXIV

THE OARSMEN

Do you hear the tumult of death afar,
The call midst the fire-floods and poisonous clouds
--The Captain's call to the steersman to turn the ship to an unnamed shore,
For that time is over--the stagnant time in the port--
Where the same old merchandise is bought and sold in an endless round,
Where dead things drift in the exhaustion and emptiness of truth.

They wake up in sudden fear and ask,
"Comrades, what hour has struck?
When shall the dawn begin?"
The clouds have blotted away the stars--
Who is there then can see the beckoning finger of the day?
They run out with oars in hand, the beds are emptied, the mother prays, the wife watches by the door;
There is a wail of parting that rises to the sky,
And there is the Captain's voice in the dark:
"Come, sailors, for the time in the harbour is over!"

All the black evils in the world have overflowed their banks,

Yet, oarsmen, take your places with the blessing of sorrow in your souls!

Whom do you blame, brothers? Bow your heads down!

The sin hás been yours and ours.

The heat growing in the heart of God for ages--

The cowardice of the weak, the arrogance of the strong, the greed of fat prosperity, the rancour of the wronged, pride of race, and insult to man--

Has burst God's peace, raging in storm.

Like a ripe pod, let the tempest break its heart into pieces, scattering thunders.

Stop your bluster of dispraise and of self-praise,

And with the calm of silent prayer on your foreheads sail to that unnamed shore.

We have known sins and evils every day and death we have known;

They pass over our world like clouds mocking us with their transient lightning laughter.

Suddenly they have stopped, become a prodigy,

And men must stand before them saying:

"We do not fear you, O Monster! for we have lived every day by conquering you,

"And we die with the faith that Peace is true, and Good is true, and true is the eternal One!"

If the Deathless dwell not in the heart of death,

If glad wisdom bloom not bursting the sheath of sorrow,

If sin do not die of its own revealment,

If pride break not under its load of decorations,

Then whence comes the hope that drives these men from their homes like stars rushing to their death in the morning light?

Shall the value of the martyrs' blood and mothers' tears be utterly lost in the dust of the earth, not buying Heaven with their price?

And when Man bursts his mortal bounds, is not the Boundless revealed that moment?

LXXXV

THE SONG OF THE DEFEATED

My Master has bid me while I stand at the roadside, to sing the song of Defeat, for that is the bride whom He woos in secret.

She has put on the dark veil, hiding her face from the crowd, but the jewel glows on her breast in the dark.

She is forsaken of the day, and God's night is waiting for her with its lamps lighted and flowers wet with dew.

She is silent with her eyes downcast; she has left her home behind her, from her home has come that wailing in the wind.

But the stars are singing the love-song of the eternal to a face sweet with shame and suffering.

The door has been opened in the lonely chamber, the call has sounded, and the heart of the darkness throbs with awe because of the coming tryst.

LXXXVI

THANKSGIVING

Those who walk on the path of pride crushing the lowly life under their tread, covering the tender green of the earth with their footprints in blood;

Let them rejoice, and thank thee, Lord, for the day is theirs.

But I am thankful that my lot lies with the humble who suffer and bear the burden of power, and hide their faces and stifle their sobs in the dark.

For every throb of their pain has pulsed in the secret depth of thy night, and every insult has been gathered into thy great silence. And the morrow is theirs.

O Sun, rise upon the bleeding hearts blossoming in flowers of the morning, and the torchlight revelry of pride shrunken to ashes.

GITANJALI

I

THOU HAST made me endless, such is thy pleasure. This frail vessel thou emptiest again and again, and fillest it ever with fresh life.

This little flute of a reed thou hast carried over hills and dales, and hast breathed through it melodies eternally new.

At the immortal touch of thy hands my little heart loses its limits in joy and gives birth to utterance ineffable.

Thy infinite gifts come to me only on these very small hands of mine. Ages pass, and still thou pourest, and still there is room to fill.

WHEN THOU commandest me to sing it seems that my heart would break with pride; and I look to thy face, and tears come to my eyes.

All that is harsh and dissonant in my life melts into one sweet harmony—and my adoration spreads wings like a glad bird on its flight across the sea.

I know thou takest pleasure in my singing. I know that only as a singer I come before thy presence.

I touch by the edge of the far spreading wing of my song thy feet which I could never aspire to reach.

Drunk with the joy of singing I forget myself and call three friend who art my lord.

I KNOW not how thou singest, my master! I ever listen in silent amazement.

The light of thy music illumines the world. The life breath of thy music runs from sky to sky. The holy stream of thy music breaks through all stony obstacles and rushes on.

My heart longs to join in thy song, but vainly struggles for a voice. I would speak, but speech breaks not into song, and I cry out baffled. Ah, thou hast made my heart captive in the endless meshes of thy music, my master!

MY SONG has put off her adornments. She has no pride of dress and decoration. Ornaments would mar our union; they would come between thee and me; their jingling would drown thy whispers.

My poet's vanity dies in shame before thy sight. O master poet, I have sat down at thy feet Only let me make my life simple and straight, like a flute of reed for thee to fill with music.

LEAVE this chanting and singing and telling of beads! Whom dost thou worship in this lonely dark corner of a temple with doors all shut? Open thine eyes and see thy God is not before thee!

He is there were where the tiller is tilling the hard ground and where the path-maker is breaking stones. He is with them in sun and in shower, and his garment is covered with dust Put off thy holy mantle and even like him come down on the dusty soil!

Deliverance? Where is this deliverance to be found? Our master himself has joyfully taken upon him the bonds of creation; he is bound with us all for ever.

Come out of thy meditations and leave aside thy flowers and incense! What harm is there if thy clothes become tattered and stained? Meet him and stand by him in toil and in sweat of thy brow.

THE TIME that my journey takes is long and the way of it long.

I came out on the chariot of the first gleam of light, and pursued my voyage through the wildernesses of worlds leaving my track on many a star and planet.

It is the most distant course that comes nearest to thyself, and that training is the most intricate which leads to the utter simplicity of a tune.

The traveller has to knock at every alien door to come to his own, and one has to wander through all the outer worlds to reach the innermost shrine at the end.

My eyes strayed far and wide before I shut them and said 'Here art thou!'

The question and the cry Oh, where?' melt into tears of a thousand streams and deluge the world with the flood of the assurance I am!'

THE SONG that I came to sing remains unsung to this day.

I have spent my days in stringing and in unstringing my instrument.

The time has not come true, the words have not been rightly set; only there is the agony of wishing in my heart.

The blossom has not opened; only the wind is sighing by.

I have not seen his face, nor have I listened to his voice; only I have heard his gentle footsteps from the road before my house.

The livelong day has passed in spreading his seat on the floor; but the lamp has not been lit and I cannot ask him into my house.

I live in the hope or meeting with him; but this meeting is not yet.

CLOUDS heap upon clouds and it darkens. Ah, love, why dost thou let me wait outside at the door all alone?

In the busy moments of the noontide work I am with the crowd, but on this dark lonely day it is only for thee that I hope.

If thou showest me not thy face, if thou leavest me wholly aside, I know not how I am to pass these long, rainy hours.

I keep gazing on the far away gloom of the sky, and my heart wanders wailing with the restless wind.

IF THOU speakest not I will fill my heart with thy silence and endure it. I will keep still and wait like the night with starry vigil and its head bent low with patience.

The morning will surely come, the darkness will vanish, and thy voice pour down in golden streams breaking through the sky.

Then thy words will take wing in songs from every one of my birds nests, and thy melodies will break forth in flowers in all my forest groves.

WHERE the mind is without fear and the head is held high;

Where knowledge is free;

Where the world has not been broken up into fragments by narrow domestic walls;

Where words come out from the depth of truth;

Where tireless striving stretches its arms towards perfection;

Where the clear stream of reason has not lost its way into the dreary desert and of dead habit;

Where the mind is led forward by thee into ever-widening thought and action—

Into that heaven of freedom, my Father, let my country awake.

II

THAT I want thee, only thee—let my heart repeat without end. All desires that distract me, day and night, are false and empty to the core.

As the night keeps hidden in its gloom the petition for light, even thus in the depth of my unconsciousness rings the cry—I want thee, only thee.

As the storm still seeks its end in peace when it strikes against peace with all its might, even thus my rebellion strikes against thy love and still its cry is—I want thee, only thee.

WHEN the heart is hard and parched up, come upon me with a shower of mercy.

When grace is lost from life, come with a burst of song.

When tumultuous work raises its din on all sides shutting me out from beyond, come to me, my lord of silence, with thy peace and rest.

When my beggarly heart sits crouched, shut up in a corner, break open the door, my king, and come with the ceremony of a king.

When desire blinds the mind with delusion and dust, O thou holy one, thou wakeful, come with thy light and thy thunder.

EARLY in the day it was whispered that we should sail in

a boat, only thou and I, and never a soul in the world would know of this our pilgrimage to no country and to no end.

In that shoreless ocean, at thy silently listening smile my songs would swell in melodies, free as waves, free from all bondage of words.

Is the time not come yet? Are there works still to do? Lo, the evening has come down upon the shore and in the fading light the seabirds come flying to their nests.

Who knows when the chains will be off, and the boat, like the last glimmer of sunset, vanish into the night?

⇝⇜

THE day was when I did not keep myself in readiness for thee; and entering my heart unbidden even as one of the common crowd, unknown to me, my king, thou didst press the signet of eternity upon many a fleeting moment of my life.

And to-day when by chance I light upon them and see thy signature, I find they have lain scattered in the dust mixed with the memory of joys and sorrows of my trivial days forgotten.

Thou didst not turn in contempt from my childish play among dust, and the steps that I heard in my playroom are the same that are echoing from star to star.

⇝⇜

THIS is my delight, thus to wait and watch at the wayside where shadow chases light and the rain comes in the wake of the summer.

Messengers, with tidings from unknown skies, greet me

and speed along the road. My heart is glad within, and the breath of the passing breeze is sweet.

From dawn till dusk I sit here before my door, and I know that of a sudden the happy moment will arrive when I shall see. In the meanwhile I smile and I sing all alone.

In the meanwhile the air is filling with the perfume of promise.

III

I KNOW NOT from what distant time thou art ever coming nearer to meet me. Thy sun and stars can never keep thee hidden from me for aye.

In many a morning and eve thy footsteps have been heard and thy messenger has come within my heart and called me in secret.

I know not why to-day my life is all astir, and a feeling of tremulous joy is passing through my heart.

It is as if the time were come to wind up my work, and I feel in the air a faint smell of thy sweet presence.

I HAD GONE a-begging from door to door in the village path, when thy golden chariot appeared in the distance like a gorgeous dream and I wondered who was this King of all kings!

My hopes rose high and methought my evil days were at an end, and 1 stood waiting for alms to be given unasked and for wealth scattered on all sides in the dust.

The chariot stopped where I stood. Thy glance fell on me and thou camest down with a smile. I felt that the luck of my life had come at last. Then of a sudden thou didst hold out thy right hand and say 'What hast thou to give to me?'

Ah, what a kingly jest was it to open thy palm to a beggar to beg! I was confused and stood undecided, and then from my wallet I slowly took out the least little grain of corn and gave it to thee.

But how great my surprise when at the day's end I emptied my bag on the floor to find a least little grain of gold among the poor heap. I bitterly wept and wished that I had had the heart to give thee my all.

THE NIGHT darkened. Our day's works had been done. We thought that the last guest had arrived for the night and the doors in the village were all shut. Only some said, The king was to come. We laughed and said 'No, it cannot be!

It seemed there were knocks at the door and we said it was nothing but the wind. We put out the lamps and lay down to sleep. Only some said, 'It is the messenger!' We laughed and said 'No, it must be the wind!'

There came a sound in the dead of the night. We sleepily thought it was the distant thunder. The earth shook, the walls rocked, and it troubled us in our sleep. Only some said, it was the sound of wheels. We said in a drowsy murmur, 'No, it must be the rumbling of clouds!'

The night was still dark when the drum sounded. The voice came 'Wake up! delay not!' We pressed our hands on our hearts and shuddered with fear. Some said, 'Lo, there is the king's flag!' We stood up on our feet and cried 'There is no time for delay!'

The king has come—but where are lights, where are wreaths? Where is the throne to seat him? Oh, shame, Oh utter shame! Where is the hall, the decorations? Some one has said, 'Vain is this cry! Greet him with empty hands, lead him into thy rooms all bare!'

Open the doors, let the conch-shells be sounded! In the depth of the night has come the king of our dark, dreary house. The thunder roars in the sky. The darkness shudders with lightning. Bring out thy tattered piece of mat and spread it in the courtyard. With the storm has come of a sudden our king of the fearful night.

I ASKED nothing from thee; I uttered not my name to thine ear. When thou took'st thy leave I stood silent. I was alone by the well where the shadow of the tree fell aslant, and the women had gone home with their brown earthen pitchers full to the brim. They called me and shouted, 'Come with us, the morning is wearing on to noon.' But I languidly lingered awhile lost in the midst of vague musings.

I heard not thy steps as thou camest. Thine eyes were sad when they fell on me; thy voice was tired as thou spokest low—'Ah, I am a thirsty traveller.' I started up from my day-dreams and poured water from my jar on thy joined palms. The leaves rustled overhead; the cuckoo sang from the unseen dark, and perfume of *babla* flowers came from the bend of the road.

I stood speechless with shame when my name thou didst ask. Indeed, what had I done for thee to keep me in remembrance? But the memory that I could give water to thee to allay thy thirst will cling to my heart and enfold it in sweetness. The morning hour is late, the bird sings in weary notes, *neem* leaves rustle overhead and I sit and think and think.

⁂

LET ALL THE strains of joy mingle in my last song—the joy that makes the earth flow over in the riotous excess of the grass, the joy that sets the twin brothers, life and death, dancing over the wide world, the joy that sweeps in with the tempest, shaking and waking all life with laughter, the joy that sits still with its tears on the open red lotus of pain, and the joy that throws everything it has upon the dust, and knows not a word.

⁂

ON THE seashore of endless worlds children meet. The infinite sky is motionless overhead and the restless water is boisterous. On the seashore of endless worlds the children meet with shouts and dances.

They build their houses with sand and they play with empty shells. With withered leaves they weave their boats and smilingly float them on the vast deep. Children have their play on the seashore of worlds.

They know not how to swim, they know not how to cast nets. Pearl fishers dive for pearls, merchants sail in their ships, while children gather pebbles and scatter them again. They seek not for hidden treasures, they know not how to cast nets.

The sea surges up with laughter and pale gleams the smile of the sea beach. Death-dealing waves sing meaningless ballads to the children, even like a mother while rocking her baby's cradle. The sea play with children, and pale gleams the smile of the sea beach.

On the seashore of endless worlds children meet. Tempest roams in the pathless sky, ships get wrecked in the trackless water, death is abroad and children play. On the seashore of endless worlds is the great meeting of children.

⁂

WHEN I BRING to you coloured toys, my child, I understand why there is such a play of colours on clouds, on water, and why flowers are painted in tints—when I give coloured toys to you, my child.

When I sing to make you dance I truly know why there is music in leaves, and why waves send their chorus of voices to the heart of the listening earth—when I sing to make you dance.

When I bring sweet things to your greedy hands I know why there is honey in the cup of the flower and why fruits are secretly filled with sweet juice— when I bring sweet things to your greedy hands.

When I kiss your face to make you smile, my darling, I surely understand what the pleasure is that streams from the sky in morning light, and what delight that is which the summer breeze brings to my body—when I kiss you to make you smile.

⁂

THOU HAST made me known to friends whom I knew not. Thou hast given me seats in homes, not my own. Thou hast brought the distant near and made a brother of the stranger.

I am uneasy at heart when I have to leave my accustomed

shelter; I forget that there abides the old in the new, and that there also thou abidest.

Through birth and death, in this world or in others, wherever thou leadest me it is thou, the same, the one companion of my endless life who ever linkest my heart with bonds of joy to the unfamiliar.

When one knows thee, then alien there is none, then no door is shut. Oh, grant me my prayer that I may never lose the bliss of the touch of the one in the play of the many.

ON THE SLOPE of the desolate river among tall grasses I asked her, 'Maiden, where do you go shading your lamp with your mantle? My house is all dark and lonesome—lend me your light!' She raised her dark eyes for a moment and looked at my face through the dusk. 'I have come to the river,' she said, 'to float my lamp on the stream when the daylight wanes in the west.' I stood alone among tall grasses and watched the timid flame of her lamp uselessly drifting in the tide.

In the silence of gathering night I asked her, 'Maiden, your lights are all lit—then where do you go with your lamps? My house is all dark and lonesome,— lend me your light.' She raised her dark eyes on my face and stood for a moment doubtful. 'I have come,' she said at last, 'to dedicate my lamp to the sky.' I stood and watched her light uselessly burning in the void.

In the moonless gloom of midnight I asked her, 'Maiden, what is your quest holding the lamp near your hear? My house is all dark and lonesome,— lend me your light.' She stopped for a minute and thought and gazed at my face in the dark. 'I have brought my light,' she said, 'to join the carnival of lamps.' I stood and watched her little lamp uselessly lost among lights.

THOU ART THE sky and thou art the nest as well. O thou beautiful, there in the nest it is thy love that encloses the soul with colours and sounds and odours.

There comes the morning with the golden basket in her right hand bearing the wreath of beauty, silently to crown the earth.

And there comes the evening over the lonely meadows deserted by herds, through trackless paths, carrying cool draughts of peace in her golden pitcher from the western ocean of rest.

But there, where spreads the infinite sky for the soul to take her flight in, reigns the stainless white radiance. There is no day nor night, nor form nor colour, and never, never a word.

IV

THE SAME stream of life that runs through my veins night and day runs through the world and dances in rhythmic measures.

It is the same life that shoots in joy through the dust of the earth in numberless blades of grass and breaks into tumultuous waves of leaves and flowers.

It is the same life that is rocked in the ocean-cradle of birth and of death, in ebb and in flow.

I feel my limbs are made glorious by the touch of this world of life. And my pride is from the life-throb of ages dancing in my blood this moment.

ON MANY AN idle day have I grieved over lost time. But it is never lost, my lord. Thou hast taken every moment of my life in thine own hands.

Hidden in the heart of things thou art nourishing seeds into sprouts, buds into blossoms, and ripening flowers into fruitfulness.

I was tired and sleeping on my idle bed and imagined all work had ceased. In the morning I woke up and found my garden full with wonders of flowers.

DEITY OF THE ruined temple! The broken strings of *Vina* sing no more your praise. The bells in the evening proclaim not your time of worship. The air is still and silent about you.

In your desolate dwelling comes the vagrant spring breeze. It brings the tidings of flowers—the flowers that for your worship are offered no more.

Your worshipper of old wanders ever longing for favour still refused. In the eventide, when fires and shadows mingle with the gloom of dust, he wearily comes back to the ruined temple with hunger in his heart.

Many a festival day comes to you in silence, deity of the ruined temple. Many a night of worship goes away with lamp unlit.

Many new images are built by masters of cunning art and carried to the holy stream of oblivion when their time is come.

Only the deity of the ruined temple remains unworshipped in deathless neglect.

I KNOW that the day will come when my sight of this earth shall be lost, and life will take its leave in silence, drawing the last curtain over my eye.

Yet stars will watch at night, and morning rise as before, and hours heave like sea waves casting up pleasures and pains.

When I think of this end of my moments, the barrier of the moments breaks and I see by the light of death thy world with its careless treasures. Rare is its lowliest seat, rare is its meanest lives.

Things that I longed for in vain and things that I got— let them pass. Let me but truly possess the things that I ever spurned and overlooked.

I HAVE got my leave. Bid me farewell, my brothers! I bow to you all and take my departure.

Here I give back the keys of my door—and I give up all claims to my house, I only ask for last kind words from you.

We were neighbours for long, but I received more than I could give. Now they day has dawned and the lamp that lit my dark corner is out. A summons has come and I am ready for my journey.

V

I WAS not aware of the moment when I first crossed the threshold of this life.

What was the power that made me open out into this vast mystery like a bud in the forest at midnight!

When in the morning I looked upon the light I felt in a moment that I was no stranger in this world, that the inscrutable without name and form had taken me in its arms in the form of my own mother.

Even so, in death the same unknown will appear as ever known to me. And because I love this life, I know I shall love death as well.

The child cries out when from the right breast the mother takes it away, in the very next moment to find in the left one its consolation.

⁂

WHEN I GO from hence let this be my parting word, that what I have seen is unsurpassable.

I have tasted of the hidden honey of this lotus that expands on the ocean of light, and thus am I blessed—let this be my parting word.

In this playhouse of infinite forms I have had my play and here have I caught sight of him that is formless.

My whole body and my limbs have thrilled with his touch who is beyond touch; and if the end comes here, let it come—let this be my parting word.

⁂

I DIVE down into the depth of the ocean of forms, hoping to gain the perfect pearl of the formless.

No more sailing from harbour to harbour with this my weather-beaten boat. The days are long passed when my sport was to be tossed on waves.

And now I am eager to die into the deathless.

Into the audience hall by the fathomless abyss where swells up the music of toneless strings I shall take this harp of my life.

I shall tune it to the notes of for ever, and, when it has sobbed out its last utterance, lay down my silent harp at the feet of the silent.

IN ONE salutation to thee, my God, let all my senses spread out and touch this world at thy feet.

Like a rain-cloud of July hung low with its burden of unshed showers let all my mind bend down at thy door in one salutation to thee.

Let all my songs, gather together their diverse strains into a single current and flow to a sea of silence in one salutation to thee.

Like a flock of homesick cranes flying night and day back to their mountain nests let all my life take its voyage to its eternal home in one salutation to thee.

STRAY BIRDS

I

STRAY birds of summer come to my window to sing and fly away.

And yellow leaves of autumn, which have no songs, flutter and fall there with a sigh.

IF YOU shed tears when you miss thc sun, you also miss the stars.

HER wistful face haunts my. dreams like the rain at night.

LISTEN, my heart, to the whispers of the world with which it makes love to you.

II

DO NOT seat your love upon a precipice because it is high.

✣

THESE LITTLE thoughts are the rustle of leaves; they have their whisper of joy in my mind.

✣

LIFE FINDS its wealth by the claims of the world, and its worth by the claims of love.

✣

DO NOT blame your food because you have no appetite.

✣

YOU SMILED and talked to me of nothing and I felt that for this I had been waiting long.

✣

THE FISH in the water is silent, the animal on the earth is noisy, the bird in the air is singing, But Man has in him the silence of the sea, the noise of the earth and the music of the air.

✣

III

I THANK thee that I am none of the wheels of power but I am one with the living creatures that are crushed by it.

⁂

LIKE THE meeting of the seagulls and the waves we meet and come near. The seagulls fly off, the waves roll away and we depart.

⁂

WE READ the world wrong and say that it deceives us.

⁂

YOUR VOICE, my friend, wanders in my heart, like me muffled sound of the sea among these listening pines.

⁂

LET LIFE be beautiful like summer flowers and death like autumn leaves.

⁂

THE HILLS are like shouts of children who raise their arms, trying to catch stars.

⁂

THIS RAINY evening the wind is restless. I look at the swaying branches and ponder over the greatness of all things.

⋙⋘

ONE SAD voice has its nest among the ruins of the years. It sings to me in the night,—'I loved you.'

⋙⋘

MY THOUGHTS shimmer with these shimmering leaves and my heart sings with the touch of this sunlight; my life is glad to be floating with all things into the blue of space, into the dark of time.

⋙⋘

IV

GOD'S GREAT power is in the gentle breeze, not in the storm.

⋙⋘

THE WORLD has kissed my soul with its pain, asking for its return in songs.

⋙⋘

WOMAN, IN your laughter you have the music of the fountain of life.

⋙⋘

A MIND all logic is like a knife all blade. It makes the hand bleed that uses it.

→←

V

MEN ARE cruel, but Man is kind.

→←

OUR NAMES are the light that glows on the sea waves at night and then dies without leaving its signature.

→←

MAN is worse than an animal when he is an animal.

→←

LET MY thoughts come to you, when I am gone, like the afterglow of sunset at the margin of starry silence.

→←

WE LIVE in this world when we love it.

LOVER'S GIFT

1

YOU allowed your kingly power to vanish, Shajahan, but your wish was to make imperishable a tear-drop of love.

Time has no pity for the human heart, he laughs at its sad struggle to remember.

You allured him with beauty, made him captive, and crowned the formless death with fadeless form.

The secret whispered in the hush of night to the ear of your love is wrought in the perpetual silence of stone.

Though empires crumble to dust, and centuries are lost in shadows, the marble still sighs to the stars, 'I remember.'

'I remember.'—But life forgets, for she has her call to the Endless: and she goes on her voyage unburdened, leaving her memories to the forlorn forms of beauty.

2

COME TO my garden walk, my love. Pass by the fervid flowers that press themselves on your sight. Pass them by, stopping at some chance joy, that like a sudden wonder of sunset illumines, yet eludes.

For love's gift is shy, it never tells its name, it flits across the shade, spreading a shiver of joy along the dust. Overtake it or miss it for ever. But a gift that can be grasped is merely a frail flower, or a lamp with. a flame that will flicker.

3

THE FRUITS come in crowds into my orchard, they jostle each other. They surge up in the light in an anguish of fullness.

Proudly step into my orchard, my queen, sit there in the shade, pluck the ripe fruits from their stems, and let them yield, to the utmost, their burden of sweetness at your lips.

In my orchard the butterflies shake their wings in the sun, the leaves tremble, the fruits clamour to come to completion.

4

SHE IS near to my heart as the meadow-flower to the earth; she is sweet to me as sleep is to tired limbs. My love for her is my life flowing in its fullness, like a river in autumn flood, running with serene abandonment. My songs are one with my love, like the murmur of a stream, that sings with all its waves and currents.

5

I WOULD ask for still more, if I had the sky with all its stars, and the world with its endless riches; but I would be content with the smallest comer of this earth if only she were mine.

6

IN THE light of this thriftless day of spring, my poet, sing of those who pass by and do not linger, who laugh as they run and never look back, who blossom in an hour of unreasoning delight, and fade in a moment without regret.

Do not sit down silently, to tell the beads of your past tears and smiles,—do not stop to pick up the dropped petals from the flowers of overnight, do not go to seek things that evade you, to know the meaning that is not plain,—leave the gaps in your life where they are, for the music to come out of their depths.

7

IT IS little that remains now, the rest was spent in one careless summer. It is just enough to put in a song and sing to you; to weave in a flower-chain gently clasping your wrist; to hang in your ear like a round pink pearl, like a blushing whisper; to risk in a game one evening and utterly lose.

My boat is a frail small thing, not fit for crossing wild waves in the rain. If you but lightly step on it I shall gently row you by the shelter of the shore, where the dark water in ripples are like a dream-ruffled sleep;

where the dove's cooing from the drooping branches makes the noonday shadows plaintive. At the day's end, when you are tired, I shall pluck a dripping lily to put in your hair and take my leave.

8

THERE IS ROOM for you. You are alone with your few sheaves of rice. My boat is crowded, it is heavily laden, but how can I turn you away? Your young body is slim and swaying; there is a twinkling smile in the edge of your eyes, and your robe is coloured like the rain-cloud.

The travellers will land for different roads and homes. You will sit for a while on the prow of my boat, and at the journey's end none will keep you back.

Where do you go, and to what home, to garner your sheaves? I will not question you, but when I fold my sails and moor my boat, I shall sit and wonder in the evening,— Where do you go, and to what home, to garner your sheaves?

9

WOMAN, your basket is heavy, your limbs are tired. For what distance have you set out, with what hunger of profit. The way is long and the dust is hot in the sun.

See, the lake is deep and full, its water dark like a crow's eye. The banks are sloping and tender with grass.

Dip your tired feet into the water. The noon-tide wind will pass its fingers through your hair; the pigeons will croon their sleep songs, the leaves will murmur the secrets that nestle in the shadows.

What matters it if the hours pass and the sun sets; if the way through the desolate land be lost in the waning light.

Yonder is my house, by the hedge of flowering *henna;* I

will guide you. I will make a bed for you, and light a lamp. In the morning when the birds are roused by the stir of milking the cows, I will waken you.

10

WHAT IS it that drives these bees from their home; these followers of unseen trails? What cry is this in their eager wings? How can they hear the music that sleeps in the flower soul? How can they find their way to the chamber where the honey lies shy and silent ?

11

IT WAS only the budding of leaves in the summer, the summer that came into the garden by the sea. It was only a stir and rustle in the south wind, a few lazy snatches of songs, and then the day was done.

But let there be flowering of love in the summer to come in the garden by the sea. Let my joy take its birth and clap its hands and dance with the surging songs, and make the morning open its eyes wide in sweet amazement.

12

AGES AGO when you opened the south gate or the garden of gods, and came down upon the first youth of the earth, O Spring; men and women rushed out of their houses, laughing and dancing, and pelting each other with flower-dust in a sudden madness of mirth.

Year-after year you bring the same flowers that you

scattered in your path in that earliest April. Therefore, to-day, in their pervading perfume, they breathe the sigh of the days that are now dreams the clinging sadness of vanished worlds. Your breeze is laden with love-legends that have faded from all human language.

One day, with fresh wonder, you came into my life that was fluttered with its first love. Since then the tender timidness of that inexperienced joy comes hidden every year in the early green buds of your lemon flowers; your red roses carry in their burning silence all that was unutterable in me: the memory of lyric hours, those days of May, rustles in the thrill of your new leaves born again and again.

13

LAST NIGHT in the garden I offered you my youth's foaming wine. You lifted the cup to your lips, you shut your eyes and smiled while I raised your veil, unbound your tresses, drawing down upon my breast your face sweet with its silence, last night when the moon's dream overflowed the world of slumber.

To-day in the dew-cooled calm of the dawn you are walking to God's temple, bathed and robed white, with a basketful of flowers in your hand. I stand aside in the shade under the tree, with my head bent, in the calm of the dawn by the lonely road to the temple.

14

IF I AM impatient to-day, forgive me, my love. It is the first summer rain, and the riverside forest is aflutter, and the blossoming *kadam* trees, are tempting the passing winds with wine-cups of perfume. See, from all corners of the sky lightnings are darting their glances, and winds are rampant in your hair.

If to-day I bring my homage to you, forgive me, my love. The everyday world is hidden in the dimness of the rain, all work has stopped in the village, the meadows are desolate. In your dark eyes the coming of the rain finds its music, and it is at your door that July waits with jasmines for your hair in its blue skirt.

15

HER NEIGHBOURS call her dark in the village-but she is a lily to my heart, yes, a lily though not fair. Light came muffled with clouds, when first I saw her in the field; her head was bare, her veil was off, her braided hair hanging loose on her neck. She may be dark as they say in the village, but I have seen her black eyes and am glad.

The pulse of the air boded storm. She rushed out of the hut, when she heard her dappled cow low in dismay. For a moment she turned her large eyes to the clouds, and felt a stir of the coming rain in the sky. I stood at the corner of the ricefield.—if she noticed me, it was known only to her (and perhaps I know it). She is dark as the message of shower in summer, dark as the shade of flowering woodland; she is dark as the longing for unknown love in the wistful night of May.

16

SHE DWELT here by the pool with its landing-stairs in ruins. Many an evening she had watched the moon made dizzy by the shaking of bamboo leaves, and on many a rainy day the smell of the wet earth had come to her over the young shoots of rice.

Her pet name is known here among those date-palm groves, and in the court-yards where girls sit and talk, while stitching their winter quilts. The water in this pool keeps in its depth the memory of her swimming limbs, and her wet feet had left their marks, day after day, on the footpath leading to the. village.

The women who come to-day with their vessels to the water, have all seen her smile over simple jests, and the old peasant, taking his bullocks to their bath, used to stop at her door every day to greet her.

Many a sailing boat passes by this village; many a traveller takes rest beneath that banyan tree; the ferry boat crosses to yonder ford carrying crowds to the market; but they never notice this spot by the village road, near the pool with its ruined landing-stairs,— where dwelt she whom I love.

17

WHILE AGES passed and the bees haunted the summer gardens, the moon smiled to the lilies of the night, the lightnings flashed their fiery kisses to the clouds and fled laughing, the poet stood in a corner, one with the trees and clouds. He kept his heart silent, like a flower, watched through his dreams as does the crescent moon; and wandered like the summer breeze for no purpose.

One April evening, when the moon rose up like a bubble from the depth of the sunset; and one maiden was busy watering the plants; and one feeding her doe, and one making her peacock dance, the poet broke out singing,—

'O listen to the secrets of the world. I know that the lily is pale for the moon's love. The lotus draws her veil aside before the morning sun, and the reason is simple if you think. The meaning of the bee's hum in the ear of the early jasmine has escaped the learned, but the poet knows.'

The sun went down in a blaze of blush, the moon loitered behind the trees, and the south wind whispered to the lotus, that the poet was not as simple as he seemed. The maidens and youths clapped their hands and cried,—'The world's secret is out.' They looked into each other's eyes and sang—'Let our secret as well be flung into the winds.'

18

YOUR DAYS will be full of cares, if you must give me your heart. My house by the cross-roads has its doors open and my mind is absent–for I sing.

I shall never be made to answer for it, if you must give me your heart. If I pledge my word to you in tunes now, and am too much in earnest to keep it when music is silent, you must forgive me; for the law laid in May is best broken in December.

Do not always keep remembering it, if you must give me your heart. When your eyes sing with love, and your voice ripples with laughter, my answers to your questions will be wild, and not miserly accurate in facts,—they are to be believed for ever and then forgotten for good.'

19

IT IS written in the book, that Man, when fifty, must leave the noisy world, to go to the forest seclusion. But the poet proclaims that only for the young is the forest hermit age. For it is the birth-place of flowers, and the haunt of birds and bees; and hidden nooks are waiting there for the thrill of lover's whispers. There the moonlight, that is all one kiss for the *malati* flowers, has its deep message, but those who understand it are far below fifty.

And alas, youth is inexperienced and wilful, therefore it is but meet, that the old should take charge of the household, and the young take to the seclusion of forest shades, and the severe discipline of courting.

20

WHERE IS the market for you, my song? Is it there where the learned muddle the summer breeze with their snuff; where dispute is unending if the oil depend upon the cask, or the cask upon the oil; where yellow manuscripts frown upon the fleet-footed frivolousness of life? My song cries out, Ah, no, no, no.

Where is the market for you, my song? Is it there where the man of fortune "grows enormous in pride and flesh in his marble palace, with his books on the shelves, dressed in leather, painted in gold, dusted by slaves, their virgin pages dedicated to the god obscure? My song gasped and said, Ah, no, no, no.

Where is the market for you, my song? Is it there where the young student sits, with his head bent upon his books, and his mind straying in youth's dreamland; where prose is prowling on the desk, and poetry hiding in the heart? There among that dusty disorder would you care to play hide-and-seek? My song remains silent in shy hesitation.

Where is the market for you, my song? Is it there where

the bride is busy in the house, where she runs to her bedroom the moment she is free, and snatches, from under her pillows, the book of romance so roughly handled by the baby, so full of the scent of her hair? My song heaves a sigh and trembles with uncertain desire.

Where is the market for you, my song? Is it there where the least of a bird's notes is never missed, where the stream's babbling finds its full wisdom, where all the lute-strings of the world shower their music upon two fluttering hearts? My song bursts out and cries, Yes, yes.

21

(From the Bengali of Devendranath Sen)

METHINKS, my love, before the daybreak of life you stood under some waterfall of happy dreams, filling your blood with its liquid turbulence. Or, perhaps, your path was through the garden of the gods, where the merry multitude of jasmine, lilies, and oleanders fell in your arms in heaps, and entering your heart became boisterous.

Your laughter is a song whose words are drowned in the clamour of tune, a rapture of odour of flowers that are not seen; it is like the moonlight breaking through your lips' window when the moon is hiding in your heart. I ask for no reason, I forget the cause, I only know that your laughter is the tumult of insurgent life.

22

I SHALL gladly suffer the pride of culture to die out in my house, if only in some fortunate future I am born a herd boy in the Brinda forest.

The herd boy who grazes his cattle sitting under the banyan tree, and idly weaves *gunja* flowers into garlands, who loves to splash and plunge in the Jamuna's cool deep stream.

He calls his companions to wake up when morning dawns, and all the houses in the lane hum with the sound of the churn, clouds of dust are raised by the cattle, the maidens come out in the courtyard to milk the kine.

As the shadows deepen under the *tomal* trees, and the dusk gathers on the river-banks; when the milkmaids, while crossing the turbulent water tremble with fear; and loud peacocks, with tails outspread, dance in the forest, he watches the summer clouds.

When the April night is sweet as a fresh-blown flower, he disappears in the forest with a peacock's plume in his hair; the swing ropes are twined with flowers on the branches; the south wind throbs with music, and the merry shepherd boys crowd on the banks of the blue river.

No, I will never be the leader, brothers, of this new age of new Bengal; I shall not trouble to light the lamp of culture for the benighted. If only I could be born, under the shady Ashoka groves, in some village of Brinda, where milk is churned by the maidens.

23

I LOVED the sandy bank where, in the lonely pools, ducks clamoured and turtles basked in the sun; where, with evening, stray fishing-boats took shelter in the shadow by the tall grass.

You loved the wooded bank where shadows were gathered in the arms of the bamboo thickets; where women came with their vessels through the winding lane.

The same river flowed between us, singing the same song to both its banks. I listened to it, lying alone on the sand under the stars; and you listened sitting by the edge of the slope in the early morning light. Only the words I heard from it you did not know and the secret it spoke to you was a mystery for ever to me.

24

YOUR WINDOW half opened and veil half raised you stand there waiting for the bangle-seller to come with his tinsel. You idly watch the heavy cart creak on in the dusty road, and the boat-mast crawling along the horizon across the far-off river.

The world to you is like an old woman's chant at her spinning-wheel, unmeaning rhymes crowded with random images.

But who knows if he is on his way this lazy sultry noon, the Stranger, carrying his basket of strange wares.

He will pass by your door with his clear cry, and you shall fling open your window, cast off your veil, come out of the dusk of your dreams and meet your destiny.

25

I CLASP your hands, and my heart plunges into the dark of your eyes, seeking you, who ever evade me behind words and silence.

Yet I know that I must be content in my love, with what is fitful and fugitive. For we have met for a moment in the crossing of the roads. Have I the power to carry you through this crowd of worlds, through this maze of paths? Have I the food that can sustain you, across the dark passage gaping with arches of death?

26

IF, BY chance you think of me, I shall sing to you when the rainy evening loosens her shadows upon the river, slowly trailing her dim light towards the west,— when the day's remnant is too narrow for work or for play.

You will sit alone in the balcony of the south, and I shall sing from the darkened room. In the growing dusk, the smell of the wet leaves will come through the window; and the stormy winds will become clamorous in the coconut grove.

When the lighted lamp is brought into the room I shall go. And then, perhaps, you will listen to the night, and hear my song when I am silent.

27

I FILLED my tray with whatever I had, and gave it to you. What shall I bring to your feet tomorrow, I wonder. I am like the tree that, at the end of the flowering summer, gazes at the sky with its lifted branches bare of their blossoms.

But in all my past offerings is there not a single flower made fadeless by the eternity of tears?

Will you remember it and thank me with your eyes when I stand before you with empty hands at the leave-taking of my summer days?

28

I DREAMT that she sat by my head, tenderly ruffling my hair with her fingers, playing the melody of her touch. I looked at her face and struggled with my tears, till the agony of unspoken words burst my sleep like a bubble.

I sat up and saw the glow of the milky way above my window, like a world of silence on fire, and I wondered if at this moment she had a dream that rhymed with mine.

29

I THOUGHT I had something to say to her when our eyes met across the hedge. But she passed away. And it rocks day and night, like a boat, on every wave of the hours the word that I had to say to her. It seems to sail in the autumn clouds in an endless quest and to bloom into evening flowers seeking its lost moment in the sunset. It twinkles like fireflies in my heart to find its meaning in the dusk of despair the word that I had to say to her.

30

THE SPRING flowers break out like the passionate pain of unspoken love. With their breath comes the memory of my old day songs. My heart of a sudden has put on green leaves of desire. My love came not but her touch is in my limbs, and her voice comes across the fragrant fields. Her gaze is in the sad depth of the sky, but where are her eyes? Her kisses flit in the air, but where are her lips?

31

A POSY

MY flowers were like milk and honey and wine; I bound them into a posy with a golden ribbon, but they escaped my watchful care and fled away and only the ribbon remains.

My songs were like milk and honey and wine, they were held in the rhythm of my beating heart, but they spread their wings and fled away, the darlings of the idle hours, and my heart beats in silence.

The beauty I loved was like milk and honey" and wine, her lips like the rose of the dawn, her eyes bee-black. I kept my heart silent lest it should startle her, but she eluded me like my flowers and like my songs, and my love remains alone.

32

MANY A TIME when the spring day knocked at our door I kept busy with my work and you did not answer. Now when I am left alone and heartsick the spring day comes once again, but I know not how to turn him away from the door. When he came to crown us with joy the gate was shut, but now when he comes with his gift of sorrow his path must be open.

33

THE BOISTEROUS spring, who once came into my life with its lavish laughter, burdening her hours with improvident roses, setting skies aflame with the red kisses of new-born *ashoka* leaves, now comes stealing into my solitude through the lonely lanes along the brooding shadows heavy with silence, and sits still in my balcony gazing across the fields, where the green of the earth swoons exhausted in the utter paleness of the sky.

34

WHEN OUR farewell moment came, like a low-hanging rain cloud, I had only time to tie a red ribbon on your wrist, while my hands trembled. Today I sit alone on the grass in the season of *mahua* flowers, with one quivering question in my mind, 'Do you still keep the little red ribbon tied on your wrist?'

You went by the narrow road that skirted the blossoming field of flax. I saw that my garland of overnight was still hanging loose from your hair. But why did you not wait till I could gather, in the morning, new flowers for my final gift? I wonder if unaware it dropped on your way,—the garland hanging loose from your hair.

Many a song I had sung to you, morning and evening, and the last one you carried in your voice when you went away. You never tarried to hear the one song unsung I had for you alone and for. ever. I wonder if, at last, you are tired of my song that you hummed to yourself while walking through the field.

35

LAST NIGHT clouds were threatening and *amlak* branches struggled in the grips of the gusty wind. I hoped, if dreams came to me, they would come in the shape of my beloved, in the lonely night loud with rain.

The winds still moan through the fields, and the tear-stained cheeks of dawn are pale. My dreams have been in vain, for truth is hard, and dreams, too, have their own ways.

Last night when the darkness was drunken with storm, and the rain, like night's veil, was torn by the winds into shreds, would it make truth jealous, if untruth came to me in the shape of my beloved, in the starless night loud with rain?

36

MY FETTERS, you made music in my heart. I played with you all day long and made you my ornament. We were the best of friends, my fetters. There were times when I was afraid of you, but my fear made me love you the more. You were companions of my long dark night, and I make my bow to you, before I bid you good-bye, my fetters.

37

YOU HAD your rudder broken many a time, my boat, and your sails torn to tatters. Often had you drifted towards the sea, dragging anchor and heeded not. But now there has spread a crack in your hull and your hold is heavy. Now is the time for you to end your voyage, to be rocked into sleep by the lapping of the water by the beach.

Alas, I know all warning is vain. The veiled face of dark doom lures you. The madness of the storm and the waves is upon you. The music of the tide is rising high. You are shaken by the fever of that dance.

Then break your chain, my boat, and be free, and fearlessly rush to your wreck.

38

THE CURRENT in which I drifted ran rapid and strong when I was young. The spring breeze was spendthrift of itself, the trees were on fire with flowers; and the birds never slept from singing.

I sailed with giddy speed, carried away by the flood of passion; I had no time to see and feel and take the world into my being.

Now that youth has ebbed and I am stranded on the bank, I can hear the deep music of all things, and the sky opens to me its heart of stars.

39

THERE IS a looker-on who sits behind my eyes. It seems he has seen things in ages and worlds beyond memory's shore, and those forgotten sights glisten on the grass, and shiver on the leaves. He has seen under new veils the face of the one beloved, in twilight hours of many a nameless star. Therefore his sky seems to ache with the pain of countless meetings and partings, and a longing pervades this spring breeze,—the longing that is full of the whisper of ages without beginning.

40

A MESSAGE came from my youth of vanished days, saying, 'I wait for you among the quiverings of unborn May, where smiles ripen for tears and hours ache with songs unsung.'

It says, 'Come to me across the worn-out track of age, through the gates of death. For dreams fade, hopes fail, the gathered fruits of the year decay, but I am the eternal truth, and you shall meet me again and again in your voyage of life from shore to shore.'

41

THE GIRLS are out to fetch water from the river— their laughter comes through the trees, I long to join them in the lane, where goats graze in the shade, and squirrels flit from sun to shadow, across the fallen leaves.

But my day's task is already done, my jars are filled. I stand at my door to watch the glistening green of the *areca* leaves, and hear the laughing women going to fetch water from the river.

It has ever been dear to me to carry the burden of my full vessel day after day, in the dew-dipped morning freshness and in the tired glimmer of the dayfall.

Its gurgling water babbled to me when my mind was idle, it laughed with the silent laughter of my joyous thoughts— it spoke to my heart with tearful sobs when I was sad. I have carried it in stormy days, when the loud rain drowned the anxious cooing of doves.

My day's task is done, my jars are filled, the light wanes in the west, and shadows gather beneath the trees; a sigh comes from the flowering linseed field, and my wistful eyes follow the lane, that runs through the village to the bank of the dark water.

42

ARE YOU a mere picture, and not as true as those stars, true as this dust? They throb with the pulse of things, but you are immensely aloof in your stillness, painted form.

The day was when you walked with me, your breath

warm, your limbs singing of life. My world found its speech in your voice, and touched my heart with your face. You suddenly stopped in your walk, in the shadow-side of the Forever, and I went on alone.

Life, like a child, laughs, shaking its rattle of death as it runs; it beckons me on, I follow the unseen; but you stand there, where you stopped behind that dust and those stars; and you are a mere picture.

No, it cannot be. Had the life flood utterly stopped in you, it would stop the river in its flow, and the footfall of dawn in her cadence of colours. Had the glimmering dusk of your hair vanished in the hopeless dark, the woodland shade of summer would die with its dreams.

Can it be true that I forgot you? We haste on without heed, forgetting the flowers on the roadside hedge. Yet they breathe unaware into our forgetfulness, filling it with music. You have moved from my world, to take seat at the root of my life, and therefore is this forgetting—remembrance lost in its own depth.

You are no longer before my songs, but one with them. You came to me with the first ray of dawn. I lost you with the last gold of evening. Ever since I am always finding you through the dark. No, you are no mere picture.

43

DYING, YOU have left behind you the great sadness of the Eternal in my life. You have painted my thought's horizon with the sunset colours of your departure, leaving a track of tears across the earth to love's heaven. Clasped in your dear arms, life and death united in me in a marriage bond.

I think I can see you watching there in the balcony with your lamp lighted, where the end and the beginning of all things meet. My world went hence through the doors that you opened—you holding the cup of death to my lips, filling it with life from your own.

44

WHEN IN your death you died to all that was outside me, vanishing from the thousand things of the world, to be fully reborn in my sorrow, I felt that my life had grown perfect, the man and the woman becoming one in me for ever.

45

BRING BEAUTY and order into my forlorn life, woman, as you brought them into my house when you lived. Sweep away the dusty fragments of the hours, fill the empty jars and mend all neglects. Then open the inner door of the shrine, light the candle, and let us meet there in silence before our God.

46

THE SKY gazes on its own endless blue and dreams. We clouds are its whims, we have no home. The stars shine on the crown of Eternity. Their records are permanent, while ours are penciled, to be rubbed off the next moment Our part is to appear on the stage of the air to sound our tambourines and fling flashes of laughter. But from our laughter comes the rain, which is real enough, and thunder which is no jest. Yet we have no claim upon Time for wages, and the breath that blew us into being blows us away before we are given a name.

47

THE ROAD is my wedded companion. She speaks to me under my feet all day, she sings to my dreams all night.

My meeting with her had no beginning, it begins endlessly at each daybreak, renewing its summer in fresh flowers and songs, and her every new kiss is the first kiss to me.

The road and I are lovers. I change my dress for her night after night, leaving the tattered cumber of the old in the wayside inns when the day dawns.

48

I TRAVELLED the old road every day, I took my fruits to the market, my cattle to the meadows, I ferried my boat across the stream and all the ways were well known to me.

One morning my basket was heavy with wares. Men were busy in the fields, the pastures crowded with cattle; the breast of earth heaved with the mirth of ripening rice.

Suddenly there was a tremor in the air, and the sky seemed to kiss me on my forehead. My mind started up like the morning out of mist.

I forgot to follow the track. I stepped a few paces from the path, and my familiar world appeared strange to me, like a flower I had only known in bud.

My everyday wisdom was ashamed. I went astray in the

fairyland of things. It was the best luck of my life, that I lost my path that morning, and found my eternal childhood.

49

WHERE IS heaven? you ask me, my child,—the sages tell us it is beyond the limits of birth and death, unswayed by the rhythm of day and night; it is not of this earth.

But your poet knows that its eternal hunger is for time and space, and it strives evermore to be born in the fruitful dust. Heaven is fulfilled in your sweet body, my child, in your palpitating heart.

The sea is beating its drums in joy, the flowers are a-tiptoe to kiss you. For heaven is born in you, in the arms of the mother-dust.

50

CHAMPA

(Translated from the Bengali of Satyendranath Datta)

I OPENED my bud when April breathed her last and the summer scorched with kisses the unwilling earth. I came half afraid and half curious, like a mischievous imp peeping at a hermit's cell.

I heard the frightened whispers of the despoiled woodland, and the *Kokil* gave voice to the languor of the summer; through the fluttering leaf curtain of my birth-chamber I saw the world grim, grey, and haggard.

Yet boldly I came out strong with the faith of youth, quaffed the fiery wine from the glowing bowl of the sky, and proudly saluted the morning, I, the champa flower, who carry the perfume of the sun in my heart.

54

IN THE BEGINNING of time, there rose from the churning of God's dream two women. One is the dancer at the court of paradise, the desired of men, she who laughs and plucks the minds of the wise from their cold meditations and of fools from their emptiness; and scatters them like seeds with careless hands in the extravagant winds of March, in the flowering frenzy of May.

The other is the crowned queen of heaven, the mother, throned on the fullness of golden autumn; she who in the harvest-time brings straying hearts to the smile sweet as tears, the beauty deep as the sea of silence,—brings them to the temple of the Unknown, at the holy confluence of Life and Death.

55

THE NOONDAY air is quivering, like gauzy wings of a dragon-fly. Roofs of the village huts brood bird like over the drowsy households, while a *Kokil* sings unseen from its leafy loneliness.

The fresh liquid notes drop upon the tuneless toil of the human crowd, adding music to lovers' whispers, to mothers' kisses, to children's laughter. They flow over our thoughts, like a stream over pebbles, rounding them in beauty every unconscious moment.

56

THE EVENING was lonely for me, and I was reading a book till my heart became dry, and it seemed to me that beauty was a thing fashioned by the traders in words. Tired I shut the book and snuffed the candle. In a moment the room was flooded with moonlight.

Spirit of Beauty, how could you, whose radiance over brims the sky, stand hidden behind a candle's tiny flame? How could a few vain words from a book rise like a mist, and veil her whose voice has hushed the heart of earth into ineffable calm?

This autumn is mine, for she was rocked in my heart. The glistening bells of her anklets rang in my blood, and her misty veil fluttered in my breath. I know the touch of her blown hair in all my dreams. She is abroad in the trembling leaves that danced in my life-throbs, and her eyes that smile from the blue sky drank their light from me.

58

THINGS THRONG and laugh loud in the sky; the sands and dust dance and whirl like children. Man's mind is aroused by their shouts; his thoughts long to be the playmates of things.

Our dreams, drifting in the stream of the vague, stretch their arms to clutch the earth,—their efforts stiffen into bricks and stones, and thus the city of man is built.

Voices come swarming from the past,—seeking answers from the living moments. Beats of their wings fill the air with tremulous shadows, and sleepless thoughts in our minds leave their nests to take flight across the desert of dimness, in the passionate thirst for forms. They are lampless pilgrims, seeking the shore of light, to find themselves in things. They will be lured into poet's rhymes, they will be housed in the towers of the town not yet planned, they have their call to arms from the battlefields of the future, they are bidden to join hands in the strifes of peace yet to come.

59

THEY DO not build high towers in the Land of All-I-Have-Found. A grassy lawn runs by the road, with a stream of fugitive water at its side. The bees haunt the cottage porches abloom with passion flowers. The men set out on their errands with a smile, and in the evening they come home with a song, with no wages, in the Land of All-I-Have-Found.

In the midday, sitting in the cool of their courtyards, the women hum and spin at their wheels, while over the waving harvest comes wafted the music of shepherds' flutes. It rejoices the wayfarers' hearts who walk singing through the shimmering shadows of the fragrant forest in the Land of All-I-Have-Found.

The traders sail with their merchandise down the river, but they do not moor their boats in this land; soldiers march with banners flying, but the king never stops his chariot. Travellers who come from afar to rest here awhile, go away without knowing what there is in the Land of All-I-Have-Found.

Here crowds do not jostle each other in the roads. O poet, set up your house in this land. Wash from your feet the dust of distant wanderings, tune your lute, and at the day's end stretch yourself on the cool grass under the evening star in the Land of All-I-Have-Found.

60

TAKE BACK your coins, King's Councillor. I am of those women you sent to the forest shrine to decoy the young ascetic who had never seen a woman. I failed in your bidding.

Dimly day was breaking when the hermit boy came to bathe in the stream, his tawny locks crowded on his shoulders, like a cluster of morning clouds, and his limbs shining like a streak of sunbeam. We laughed and sang as we rowed in our boat; we jumped into the river in a mad frolic, and danced around him, when the sun rose staring at us from the water's edge in a flush of divine anger.

Like a child-god, the boy opened his eyes and watched our movements, the wonder deepening till his eyes shone like morning stars. He lifted his clasped hands and chanted a hymn of praise in his bird-like young voice, thrilling every leaf of the forest. Never such words were sung to a mortal woman before; they were like the silent hymn to the dawn which rises from the hushed hills. The women hid their mouths with their hands, their bodies swaying with laughter, and a spasm of doubt ran across his face. Quickly came I to his side, sorely pained, and, bowing to his feet, I said, 'Lord, accept my service.'

I led him to the grassy bank, wiped his body with the end of my silken mantle, and, kneeling on the ground, I dried his feet with my trailing hair. When I raised my face and looked into his eyes, I thought I felt the world's first kiss to the first woman,—Blessed am I, blessed is God, who made me a woman. I heard him say to me, 'What God unknown are you? Your touch is the touch of the Immortal, your eyes have the mystery of the midnight.'

Ah, no, not that smile, King's Councillor,—the dust of worldly wisdom has covered your sight, old man. But this boy's innocence pierced the mist and saw the shining truth, the woman divine.

Ah, how the goddess wakened in me, at the awful light of that first adoration. Tears filled my eyes, the morning ray caressed my hair like a sister, and the woodland breeze kissed my forehead as it kisses the flowers.

The women clapped their hands, and laughed their obscene laugh, and with veils dragging on the dust and hair hanging loose, they began to pelt him with flowers.

Alas, my spotless sun, could not my shame weave fiery mist to cover you in its folds? I fell at his feet and cried, 'Forgive me.' I fled like a stricken deer through shade and sun, and cried as I fled, 'Forgive me.' The women's foul laughter pressed me like a crackling fire, but the words ever rang in my ears, 'What God unknown are you?'

THE FUGITIVE

I

WE came hither together, friends, and now at the cross-roads I stop to bid you farewell.

Your path is wide and straight before you, but my call comes up by ways from the unknown.

I shall follow wind and cloud; I shall follow the stars to where day breaks behind the hills; I shall follow lovers who, as they walk, twine their days into a wreath on a single thread of song, 'I love.'

IT WAS growing dark when I asked her, 'What strange land have I come to?'

She only lowered her eyes, and the water gurgled in the throat of her jar, she walked away.

The trees hang vaguely over the bank, and the land appears as though it already belonged to the past.

The water is dumb, the bamboos are darkly still, a wristlet tinkles against the water-jar from down the lane.

Row no more, but fasten the boat to this tree,—for I love the look of this land.

The evening star goes down behind the temple dome, and the pallor of the marble landing haunts the dark water.

Belated wayfarers sigh; for light from hidden windows is splintered into the darkness by intervening wayside trees and bushes. Still that wristlet tinkles against the water-jar, and retreating steps rustle from down the lane littered with leaves.

The night deepens, the palace towers loom spectre-like, the town hums wearily.

Row no more, but fasten the boat to a tree.

Let me seek rest in this strange land, dimly lying under the stars, where darkness tingles with the tinkle of a wristlet knocking against a water-jar.

⇾⇽

O THAT I were stored with a secret, like unshed rain in summer clouds—a secret, folded up in silence, that I could wander away with.

O that I had some one to whisper to, where slow waters lap under trees that doze in the sun.

The hush this evening seems to expect a footfall, and you ask me for the cause of my tears.

I cannot give a reason why I weep, for that is a secret still withheld from me.

⇾⇽

FOR once be careless, timid traveller, and utterly lose your way; wide-awake though you are, be like broad daylight enticed by and netted in mist.

Do not shun the garden of Lost Hearts waiting at the end of the wrong road, where the grass is strewn with wrecked red flowers, and disconsolate water heaves in the troubled sea.

Long have you watched over the store gathered by weary years. Let it be stripped, with nothing remaining but the desolate triumph of losing all.

TRANSLATIONS : VAISHNAVA SONGS

I

OH SAKHI, my sorrow knows no bounds.

August comes laden with rain clouds and my house is desolate.

The stormy sky growls, the earth is flooded with rain, my love is far away, and my heart is torn with anguish.

The peacocks dance, for the clouds rumble and frogs croak.

The night brims with darkness flicked with lightning.

Vidyapati asks, 'Maiden, how are you to spend your days and nights without your lord?'

II

LUCKY was my awakening this morning, for I saw my beloved.

The sky was one piece of joy, and my life and youth were fulfilled.

To-day my house becomes my house in truth, and my body my body.

Fortune has proved a friend, and my doubts are dispelled.

Birds, sing your best; moon, shed your fairest light!

Let fly your darts, Love-God, in millions!

I wait for the moment when my body will grow golden at his touch.

Vidyapati says, 'Immense is your good fortune, and blessed is your love.'

III

I FEEL my body vanishing into the dust whereon my beloved walks.

I feel one with the water of the lake where he bathes.

Oh Sakhi, my love crosses death's boundary when I meet him.

My heart melts in the light and merges in the mirror whereby he views his face.

I move with the air to kiss him when he waves his fan, and wherever he wanders I enclose him like the sky.

Govindadas says, 'You are the gold-setting, fair maidens, he is the emerald.

⁂

IV

MY love, I will keep you hidden in my eyes; I will thread your image like a gem on my joy and hang it on my bosom.

You have been in my heart ever since I was a child, throughout my youth, throughout my life, even through all my dreams.

You dwell in my being when I sleep and when I wake.

Know that I am woman, and bear with me when you find me wanting.

For I have thought and thought and know for certain that all that is left for me in this world is your love, and if I lose you for a moment I die.

Chandidas says, 'Be tender to her who is yours in life and death.'

⁂

II

BEHIND the rusty iron gratings of the opposite window sits a girl, dark and plain of face, like a boat stranded on a sand-bank when the river is shallow in the summer.

I come back to my room after my day's work, and my tired eyes are lured to her.

She seems to me like a lake with its dark lonely waters edged by moonlight.

She has only her window for freedom: there the morning light meets her musings, and through it her dark eyes like lost stars travel back to their sky.

⪢⪡

I REMEMBER the day.

The heavy shower of rain is slackening into fitful pauses, renewed gusts of wind startle it from a first lull.

I take up my instrument. Idly I touch the strings, till, without my knowing, the music borrows the mad cadence of that storm.

I see her figure as she steals from her work, stops at my door, and retreats with hesitating steps. She comes again, stands outside leaning against the wall, then slowly enters the room and sits down. With head bent, she plies her needle in silence; but soon stops her work, and looks out of the window through the rain at the blurred line of trees.

Only this—one hour of a rainy noon filled with shadows and song and silence.

⪢⪡

WHILE stepping into the carriage she turned her head and threw me a swift glance of farewell.

This was her last gift to me. But where can I keep it safe from the trampling hours?

Must evening sweep this gleam of anguish away, as it will the last flicker of fire from the sunset?

Ought it to be washed off by the rain, as treasured pollens are from heart-broken flowers?

Leave kingly glory and the wealth of the rich to death. But may not tears keep ever fresh the memory of a glance flung through a passionate moment?

'Give it to me to keep,' said my song; 'I never touch kings' glory or the wealth of the rich, but these small things are mine for ever.'

YOU give yourself to me, like a flower that blossoms at night, whose presence is known by the dew that drips from it, by the odour shed through the darkness, as the first steps of Spring are by the buds that thicken the twigs.

You break upon my thought like waves at the high tide, and my heart is drowned under surging songs.

My heart knew of your coming, as the night feels the approach of dawn. The clouds are aflame and my sky fills with a great revealing flood.

MY songs are like bees; they follow through the air some fragrant trace—some memory—of you, to hum, around your shyness, eager for its hidden store.

When the freshness of dawn droops in the sun, when in the noon the air hangs low with heaviness and the forest is silent, my songs return home, their languid wings dusted with gold.

I THINK I shall stop startled if ever we meet after our next birth, walking in the light of a far-away world.

I shall know those dark eyes then as morning stars, and yet feel that they have belonged to some unremembered evening sky of a former life.

I shall know that the magic of your face is not all its own, but has stolen the passionate light that was in my eyes at some immemorial meeting, and then gathered from my love a mystery that has now forgotten its origin.

LAY down your lute, my love, leave your arms free to embrace me.

Let your touch bring my overflowing heart to my body's utmost brink.

Do not bend your neck and turn away your face, but offer up a kiss to me, which has been like some perfume long closed in a bud.

Do not smother this moment under vain words, but let our hearts quake in a rush of silence sweeping all thoughts to the shoreless delight.

YOU have made me great with your love, though I am but one among the many, drifting in the common tide, rocking in the fluctuant favour of the world.

You have given me a seat where poets of all time bring their tribute, and lovers with deathless names greet one another across the ages.

Men hastily pass me in the market,—never noting how my body has grown precious with your caress, how I carry your kiss within, as the sun carries in its orb the fire of the divine touch and shines for ever.

I HAVE donned this new robe to-day because my body feels like singing.

It is not enough that I am given to my love once and for ever, but out of that I must fashion new gifts every day; and shall I not seem a fresh offering, dressed in a new robe?

My heart, like the evening sky, has its endless passion for colour, and therefore I change my veils, which have now the green of the cool young grass and now that of the winter rice.

To-day my robe is tinted with the rain-rimmed blue of the sky. It brings to my limbs the colour of the boundless, the colour of the oversea hills; and it carries in its folds the delight of summer clouds flying in the wind.

I THOUGHT I would write love's words in their own colour; but that lies deep in the heart, and tears are pale.

Would you know them, friend, if the words were colourless?

I thought I would sing love's words to their own tune, but that sounds only in my heart, and my eyes are silent.

Would you know them, friend, if there were no tune?

IN the night the song came to me; but you were not there.

It found the words for which I had been seeking all day. Yes, in the stillness a moment after dark they throbbed into music, even as the stars then began to pulse with light; but you were not there. My hope was to sing it to you in the morning; but, try as I might, though the music came, the words hung back, when you were beside me.

OUR life sails on the uncrossed sea whose waves chase each other in an eternal hide-and-seek.

It is the restless sea of change, feeding its foaming flocks to lose them over and over again, beating its hands against the calm of the sky.

Love, in the centre of this circling war-dance of light and dark, yours is that green island, where the sun kisses the shy forest shade and silence is wooed by birds' singing.

III

MY HEART IS a flute he has played on. If ever it fall into other hands let him fling it away.

My lover's flute is dear to him, therefore if to-day alien breath have entered it and sounded strange notes, let him break it to pieces and strew the dust with them.

IN LOVE THE aim is neither pain nor pleasure but love only.

While free love binds, division destroys it, for love is what unites.

Love is lit from love as fire from fire, but whence came the first flame?

In your being it leaps under the rod of pain.

Then, when the hidden fire flames forth, the in and the out are one and all barriers fall in ashes.

Let the pain glow fiercely, burst from the heart and beat back darkness, need you be afraid?

The poet says, 'Who can buy love without paying its price? When you fail to give yourself you make the whole world miserly.'

⁂

EYES SEE ONLY dust and earth, but feel with the heart, and know pure joy.

The delights blossom on all sides in every form, but where is your heart's thread to make a wreath of them?

My master's flute sounds through all things, drawing me out of my lodgings wherever they may be, and while I listen I know that every step I take is in my master's house.

For he is the sea, he is the river that leads to the sea, and he is the landing-place.

⁂

I AM THE BOAT, you are the sea, and also the boatman.

Though you never make the shore, though you let me sink, why should I be foolish and afraid?

Is reaching the shore a greater prize than losing myself with you?

If you are only the haven, as they say, then what is the sea?

Let it surge and toss me on its waves, I shall be content.

I live in you whatever and however you appear. Save me or kill me as you wish, only never leave me in other hands.

IV

COME, SPRING, reckless lover of the earth, make the forest's heart pant for utterance!

Come in gusts of disquiet where flowers break open and jostle the new leaves!

Burst, like a rebellion of light, through the night's vigil, through the lake's dark dumbness, through the dungeon under the dust, proclaiming freedom to the shackled seeds!

Like the laughter of lightning, like the shout of a storm, break into the midst of the noisy town; free stifled word and unconscious effort, reinforce our flagging fight, and conquer death!

I HAVE LOOKED on this picture in many a month of March when the mustard is in bloom—this lazy line of the water and the grey of the sand beyond, the rough path along the river-bank carrying the comradeship of the field into the heart of the village.

I have tried to capture in rhyme the idle whistle of the wind, the beat of the oar-strokes from a passing boat.

I have wondered in my mind how simply it stands before me, this great world: with what fond and familiar ease it fills my heart, this encounter with the Eternal Stranger.

IN THE EVENING after they have brought their cattle home, they sit on the grass before their huts to know that you are among them unseen, to repeat in their songs the name which they have fondly given you.

While kings' crowns shine and disappear like falling stars, around village huts your name rises through the still night from the simple hearts of your lovers whose names are unrecorded.

HOW OFTEN, great Earth, have I felt my being yearn to flow over you, sharing in the happiness of each green blade that raises its signal banner in answer to the beckoning blue of the sky!

I feel as if I had belonged to you ages before I was born. That is why, in the days when the autumn light shimmers on the mellowing ears of rice, I seem to remember a past when my mind was everywhere, and even to hear voices as of playfellows echoing from the remote and deeply veiled past.

When, in the evening, the cattle return to their folds, raising dust from the meadow paths, as the moon rises higher than the smoke ascending from the village huts, I feel sad as for some great separation that happened in the first morning of existence.

V

IN THE evening my little daughter heard a call from her companions below the window.

She timidly went down the dark stairs holding a lamp in her hand, shielding it behind her veil.

I was sitting on my terrace in the star-lit night of March, when at a sudden cry I ran to see.

Her lamp had gone out in the dark spiral staircase. I asked, 'Child, why did you cry?'

From below she answered in distress, 'Father, I have lost myself!'

When I came back to the terrace under the star-lit night of March, I looked at the sky, and it seemed that a child was walking there treasuring many lamp behind her veils.

If their light went out, she would suddenly stop and a cry would sound from sky to sky, 'Father, I have lost myself!'

IN THE DEPTHS of the forest the ascetic practised penance with fast-closed eyes; he intended to deserve Paradise.

But the girl who gathered twigs brought him fruits in her skirt, and water from the stream in cups made of leaves.

The days went on, and his penance grew harsher till the fruits remained untasted, the water untouched: and the girl who gathered twigs was sad.

The Lord of Paradise heard that a man had dared to aspire to be as the Gods. Time after time he had fought the Titans, who were his peers, and kept them out of his kingdom; yet he feared a man whose power was that of suffering.

But he knew the ways of mortals, and he planned a temptation to decoy this creature of dust away from his adventure.

A breath from Paradise kissed the limbs of the girl who gathered twigs, and her youth ached with a sudden rapture of beauty, and her thoughts hummed like the bees of a rifled hive.

The time came when the ascetic should leave the forest for a mountain cave, to complete the rigour of his penance. When he opened his eyes in order to start on his journey, the girl appeared to him like a verse familiar, yet forgotten, and which an added melody made strange. The ascetic rose from his seat and told her that it was time he left the forest.

'But why rob me of my chance to serve you?' she asked with tears in her eyes.

He sat down again, thought for long, and remained on where her was.

That night remorse kept the girl awake. She began to dread her power and hate her triumph, yet her mind tossed on the waves of turbulent delight.

In the morning she came and saluted the ascetic and asked his blessing, saying she must leave him.

He gazed on her face in silence, then said, 'Go, and may your wish be fulfilled.'

For years he sat alone till his penance was complete.

The Lord of the Immortals came down to tell him that he had won Paradise.

'I no longer need it,' said he.

The God asked him what greater reward he desire.
'I want the girl who gathers twigs.'

⁂

WHEN LIKE A flaming scimitar the hill stream has been sheathed in gloom by the evening, suddenly a flock of birds passes overhead, their loud-laughing wings hurling their flight like an arrow among stars.

It startles a passion for speed in the heart of all motionless things; the hills seem to feel in their bosom the anguish of storm-clouds, and trees long to break their rooted shackles.

For me the flight of these birds has rent a veil of stillness, and reveals an immense flutter in this deep silence.

I see these hills and forests fly across time to the unknown, and darkness thrill into fire as the stars wing by.

I feel in my own being the rush of the sea-crossing bird, cleaving a way beyond the limits of life and death, while the migrant world cries with a myriad voices, 'Not here, but somewhere else, in the bosom of the Faraway.'

⁂

I FEEL THAT my heart will leave its own colour in all your scenes, O Earth, when I bid you farewell. Some notes of mine will be added to your seasons' melody, and my thoughts will breathe unrecognised through the cycle of shadows and sunshine.

In far-distant days summer will come to the lovers' garden, but they will not know that their flowers have borrowed an added beauty from my songs, nor that their love for this world has been deepened by mine.

MY EYES feel the deep peace of this sky, and there stirs through me what a tree feels when it holds out its leaves like cups to be filled with sunshine.

A thought rises in my mind, like the warm breath from grass in the sun; it mingles with the gurgle of lapping water and the sigh of weary wind in village lanes,—the thought that I have lived along with the whole life of this world and have given to it my own love and sorrows.

GIVE ME the supreme courage of love, this is my prayer—the courage to speak, to do, to suffer at thy will, to leave all things or be left alone. Strengthen me on errands of danger, honour me with pain, and help me climb to that difficult mood which sacrifices daily to thee.

Give me the supreme confidence of love, this is my prayer—the confidence that belongs to life in death, to victory in defeat, to the power hidden in frailest beauty, to that dignity in pain which accepts hurt but disdains to return it.

LAST CURTAIN

I know that the day will come
when my sight of this earth shall be lost,
and life will take its leave in silence,
drawing the last curtain over my eyes.

Yet stars will watch at night,
and morning rise as before,
and hours heave like sea waves casting up pleasures and pains.

When I think of this end of my moments,
the barrier of the moments breaks
and I see by the light of death
thy world with its careless treasures.
Rare is its lowliest seat,
rare is its meanest of lives.

Things that I longed for in vain
and things that I got
---let them pass.
Let me but truly possess

the things that I ever spurned
and overlooked.

LET ME NOT FORGET

If it is not my portion to meet thee in this life
then let me ever feel that I have missed thy sight
---let me not forget for a moment,
let me carry the pangs of this sorrow in my dreams
and in my wakeful hours.

As my days pass in the crowded market of this world
and my hands grow full with the daily profits,
let me ever feel that I have gained nothing
---let me not forget for a moment,
let me carry the pangs of this sorrow in my dreams
and in my wakeful hours.

When I sit by the roadside, tired and panting,
when I spread my bed low in the dust,
let me ever feel that the long journey is still before me
---let me not forget a moment,
let me carry the pangs of this sorrow in my dreams
and in my wakeful hours.

When my rooms have been decked out and the flutes sound
and the laughter there is loud,
let me ever feel that I have not invited thee to my house
---let me not forget for a moment,
let me carry the pangs of this sorrow in my dreams
and in my wakeful hours

❖ ❖ ❖

LEAVE THIS

Leave this chanting and singing and telling of beads!
Whom dost thou worship in this lonely dark corner of a temple with doors all shut?
Open thine eyes and see thy God is not before thee!

He is there where the tiller is tilling the hard ground
and where the pathmaker is breaking stones.
He is with them in sun and in shower,
and his garment is covered with dust.
Put off thy holy mantle and even like him come down on the dusty soil!

Deliverance?

Where is this deliverance to be found?

Our master himself has joyfully taken upon him the bonds of creation;

he is bound with us all for ever.

Come out of thy meditations and leave aside thy flowers and incense!

What harm is there if thy clothes become tattered and stained?

Meet him and stand by him in toil and in sweat of thy brow.

INNERMOST ONE

He it is, the innermost one,
who awakens my being with his deep hidden touches.

He it is who puts his enchantment upon these eyes
and joyfully plays on the chords of my heart
in varied cadence of pleasure and pain.

He it is who weaves the web of this maya
in evanescent hues of gold and silver, blue and green,
and lets peep out through the folds his feet,

at whose touch I forget myself.

Days come and ages pass,
and it is ever he who moves my heart in many a name,
in many a guise, in many a rapture of joy and of sorrow.

JOURNEY HOME

The time that my journey takes is long and the way of it long.

I came out on the chariot of the first gleam of light, and pursued my
voyage through the wildernesses of worlds leaving my track on many a star and planet.

It is the most distant course that comes nearest to thyself,
and that training is the most intricate which leads to the utter simplicity of a tune.

The traveler has to knock at every alien door to come to his own,
and one has to wander through all the outer worlds to reach the innermost shrine at the end.

My eyes strayed far and wide before I shut them and said `Here art thou!'

The question and the cry `Oh, where?' melt into tears of a thousand,
streams and deluge the world with the flood of the assurance `I am!'

❖❖❖

FOOL

O Fool, try to carry thyself upon thy own shoulders!
O beggar, to come beg at thy own door!

Leave all thy burdens on his hands who can bear all,
and never look behind in regret.

Thy desire at once puts out the light from the lamp it touches with its breath.
It is unholy---take not thy gifts through its unclean hands.
Accept only what is offered by sacred love.

❖❖❖

FAREWELL

I have got my leave. Bid me farewell, my brothers!
I bow to you all and take my departure.
Here I give back the keys of my door
---and I give up all claims to my house.
I only ask for last kind words from you.
We were neighbors for long,
but I received more than I could give.
Now the day has dawned
and the lamp that lit my dark corner is out.
A summons has come and I am ready for my journey.

❖ ❖ ❖

ENDLESS TIME

Time is endless in thy hands, my lord.
There is none to count thy minutes.
Days and nights pass and ages bloom and fade like flowers.
Thou knowest how to wait.
Thy centuries follow each other perfecting a small wild flower.
We have no time to lose,

and having no time we must scramble for a chance.
We are too poor to be late.
And thus it is that time goes by
while I give it to every querulous man who claims it,
and thine altar is empty of all offerings to the last.
At the end of the day I hasten in fear lest thy gate be shut;
but I find that yet there is time.

❖ ❖ ❖

BRINK OF ETERNITY

In desperate hope I go and search for her
in all the corners of my room;
I find her not.
My house is small
and what once has gone from it can never be regained.
But infinite is thy mansion, my lord,
and seeking her I have to come to thy door.
I stand under the golden canopy of thine evening sky
and I lift my eager eyes to thy face.
I have come to the brink of eternity from which nothing can vanish
---no hope, no happiness, no vision of a face seen through tears.
Oh, dip my emptied life into that ocean,
plunge it into the deepest fullness.

Let me for once feel that lost sweet touch
in the allness of the universe.

❖❖❖

CHAIN OF PEARLS

Mother, I shall weave a chain of pearls for thy neck
with my tears of sorrow.
The stars have wrought their anklets of light to deck thy feet,
but mine will hang upon thy breast.

Wealth and fame come from thee
and it is for thee to give or to withhold them.
But this my sorrow is absolutely mine own,
and when I bring it to thee as my offering
thou rewardest me with thy grace.
Distant Time by Rabindranath Tagore
I know not from what distant time
thou art ever coming nearer to meet me.
Thy sun and stars can never keep thee hidden from me for aye.
In many a morning and eve thy footsteps have been heard
and thy messenger has come within my heart and called me in secret.
I know not only why today my life is all astir,
and a feeling of tremulous joy is passing through my heart.

It is as if the time were come to wind up my work,
and I feel in the air a faint smell of thy sweet presence.

❖ ❖ ❖

COLORED TOYS

When I bring to you colored toys, my child,
I understand why there is such a play of colors on clouds, on water,
and why flowers are painted in tints
---when I give colored toys to you, my child.

When I sing to make you dance
I truly now why there is music in leaves,
and why waves send their chorus of voices to the heart of the listening earth
---when I sing to make you dance.

When I bring sweet things to your greedy hands
I know why there is honey in the cup of the flowers
and why fruits are secretly filled with sweet juice
---when I bring sweet things to your greedy hands.

When I kiss your face to make you smile, my darling,
I surely understand what pleasure streams from the sky in morning light,

and what delight that is that is which the summer breeze brings to my body
-when I kiss you to make you smile.

A MOMENTS INDULGENCE

I ask for a moment's indulgence to sit by thy side. The works that I have in hand I will finish afterwards.

Away from the sight of thy face my heart knows no rest nor respite, and my work becomes an endless toil in a shoreless sea of toil.

Today the summer has come at my window with its sighs and murmurs; and the bees are plying their minstrelsy at the court of the flowering grove.

Now it is time to sit quite, face to face with thee, and to sing dedication of life in this silent and overflowing leisure.